INVISIBLE FRONTLINE

TRENCH RAIDERS BOOK 3

THOMAS WOOD

BOLEYNBENNETT PUBLISHING

Copyright © 2019 by Thomas Wood

All rights reserved.

No part of this book may be reproduced in any form or by any electronic or mechanical means, including information storage and retrieval systems, without written permission from the author, except for the use of brief quotations in a book review.

This book is a work of fiction. Names, characters, places, and incidents either are products of the author's imagination or are used fictitiously. Any resemblance to actual persons, living or dead, events, or locales is entirely coincidental.
Thomas Wood

Visit my website at www.ThomasWoodBooks.com

Printed in the United Kingdom

First Printing: March 2019
by
BoleynBennett Publishing

GRAB ANOTHER BOOK FOR FREE

If you enjoy this book, why not pick up another one, completely free?

'Enemy Held Territory' follows Special Operations Executive Agent, Maurice Dumont as he inspects the defences at the bridges at Ranville and Benouville. Fast paced and exciting, this Second World War thriller is one you won't want to miss!
Details can be found at the back of this book.

1

Being a trench raider was now just as much a part of my life as breathing and eating. It wasn't so much that I was being asked to do it anymore, but it had now become a necessity in order for me to live. I had become obsessed.

I had a strange relationship with the exhilaration of it all. On the one hand, I was utterly terrified of what was waiting for me around the corner, and the other totally addicted to what I had become so good at.

It was that not knowing what was in the next dugout; maybe a hastily abandoned trench, or a well-fed and well-oiled Maxim gun, that seemed to keep my heart beating and that without it, I would die of boredom within days.

I was fully aware that my next few seconds in the German frontline could well be my last, but that was what I had begun to crave. That, and another sip from my hip flask.

That wasn't to say however, that I had become used to death and I had certainly not become desensitised to the premature end of a teenage boy. Just last week, I had found myself almost in tears, staring into the lifeless eyes of Private Paul Anderson, a young lad from Devon, who had managed to fall victim to a boobytrapped helmet that he had somehow knocked.

What had made the whole affair even more affecting was the fact that it was only the lad's second outing. He hadn't really had much of a chance to adapt or learn to what he was being asked to do.

We had been forced to leave his body in the German trench, where he would hopefully be buried on the enemy's side of the line. We were fairly confident that despite the horrific advances in being able to slaughter one another in this war, that both sides still held some regard for the sanctity of human life, in the way that we treated one another's dead.

Anderson had been absolutely dripping in blood by the time I had managed to get over to him, lethal shards of sheared artillery shell sticking out of him in every direction. The Germans must have been banking on the trench raiders to be souvenir hunters and, in Private Anderson, they had found the perfect target.

I was certain that Harry Earnshaw, the man that Anderson had replaced, would never have fallen for such a trick and cursed whatever doctor was keeping him housed up in some hospital ward. Anderson would have still been allowed to live if Harry had been with us.

Despite the constant reminders of how dangerous being in an enemy trench actually was, I began to feel far more at home in a German trench, than a British one.

Ever since the Germans had begun to launch their own retaliatory raids on the British frontline, with considerably more success than our own, the Brits back in our sector of the line had treated us with an overwhelming animosity.

We had become the antagonisers, the figures who appeared late at night to poke the enemy into action, only to retreat back to the relative safety of the nearby village. We were becoming more of an enemy to them than the Germans were. Especially because of the number of casualties the Germans were inflicting.

But there was something even more comforting in a German trench than a British one. Maybe it was the way that they were much better built, with higher parapets and more comforting sandbags. It could have had something to do with the knowledge that their dugouts were better protected from the falling shells, or the way in which that they somehow managed to keep them relatively clean. Further still, it probably had something to do with the fact that they never wanted to leave and so had transformed it into a home from home, complete with the Imperial flag that adorned many of their dugouts.

The flag that I caressed between my finger and thumb, as these thoughts paced through my mind, was battered and filthy, fraying edges and the odd hole here and there. But it still took pride of place in this dugout, nails bashed through into the wooden supports so that it would be the first thing a soldier would see when he awoke, and the last thing that he saw before he got some shut eye. It was a clever placement.

Don't be stupid. Put it down.

I repeated the reprimand to myself three or four more times as I struggled to tear myself away from the beautiful, simplistic design of the German ensign.

This is how people get killed. And not just you. The others too.

I had been perfectly conscious of the way that my mind had become distracted in the last thirty seconds or so. But, to my mind, I deserved it; I had just managed to dispose of three German soldiers before they could so much as rub their eyes as they got out of their beds.

But I was also becoming increasingly frustrated with myself for not letting the flag go. I knew I had to. For some reason, the thought that I might get myself killed wasn't troubling me as much as it previously had done.

The thought that I might simply be condemning the others also, was in fact, troubling me even less.

The more complacent I became, the easier I found it to face up to the reality that I was going to die. It was what I had been taught by a Sergeant some time ago now, but even he would have been despairing of the soldier that I had become.

Let go of it. Get on with the search.

I closed my eyes for a couple of seconds, allowing the initial wave of pain, that came with sheer exhaustion, to pass over me, before I reengaged my brain.

If you're not going to let go of it, take it. Rip it off the wall and be quick about it.

I didn't need to tell myself twice. Within a flash, the fraying, slightly stale-smelling ensign was stuffed down the front of my trousers ready for the return trip.

Now you can get on with what you are actually here for.

"Anything, Corporal?"

If Captain Arnold had come in just half a second earlier, then he would have caught me in the act of pulling the flag down, something that I knew he would stand firmly against, to the point where he probably would have had me nailing it back on the wall.

N-No, Sir," I muttered back in reply, finally pulling myself together to get on with what I was meant to be doing.

"There's got to be something here. Let's look a little more, shall we?"

He raised an accusing eyebrow in my direction and I immediately became thankful for the cork and grease packed onto my face, as my skin suddenly flashed redder than a letter box. I could tell that he could sense it, even though he wouldn't have been able to actually see the guilt that now stained my skin.

"Yes, Sir."

His eyes began darting around the small dugout, that had, until recently, housed a few sleeping soldiers as they waited for their watch. I could feel the cogs whirring in his head, like a pocket watch, as he evaluated exactly where he should begin his search to optimise the small amount of time we would have in there.

The bags that dragged his eyes downwards had grown larger and more solemn in recent weeks, as the pressures of leading this band of not-so-merry men began to weigh him down greater than a millstone. But still, he was as indefatigable as ever, moving around the dugout with agility and enthusiasm that I could only wish of having.

"Come on, Ellis. Hop to it."

I began searching anything and everything that my eyes fell on, even rummaging around in the pockets of the dead soldiers to see if there was anything of any use. My search turned up nothing apart from a few faded photographs of sweethearts and the odd carton of cigarettes, that I was quick to liberate.

"Sir, I would reckon we have about two more minutes in here. We need to wrap up shortly."

I hadn't noticed Sergeant Hughes sneaking into the dugout, but I had known that he was keeping watch outside, alongside the others, who were all crouched outside at various points trying to keep us safe.

"Thank you, Two Pews," retorted the Captain, without even looking up from the leather suitcase that he was rifling through.

He was desperate to find what we had been told might be lying around; plans for a series of underground tunnels that the Germans were hiding and living in. He had even been fairly confident that we might stumble across the entrance to the tunnels themselves, in which case he would have been the first down into the rabbit warren.

From outside, there was a dull, irregular thump, like the kind that a cricket ball makes as it lands on the other side of the boundary.

Startled at the apparent unexpected noise, Sergeant Hughes spun on his heel and scurried out of the dugout, revolver raised up high and ready for use.

I looked across at the Captain, who nodded to me and I made my way over to the entrance of the dugout to see what was going on.

I knew nothing of what went on outside the dugout, except that everything happened in the blink of an eye.

The German, who had caught Bob Sargent off guard, punched him to the ground, accounting for the dull thud that we had heard from the dugout. Bob was uninjured, apart from a broken nose and a slight momentary blackout.

The enemy soldier then progressed along the front-line trench, maybe making for his friends in the dugout, whereupon the figure of Sergeant Hughes appeared from behind the felt curtain.

The explosion of his gun lasted no longer than a third of a second, by which time he was already standing face to face with me; his third enemy soldier of the night.

I had no time to react with anything other than my instincts, as the cold steel of my sharpened bayonet was thrust into the man's chest, as I repeated the motion over and over while I tried to hit as many vital organs as I possibly could.

By the time that I relinquished my grip on the dead German, the front of his body resembled something more like a pincushion than a human chest. But still, I couldn't resist one last, fleeting thrust into the man's gut, in anticipation of the body that I would lay eyes on, upon exiting the dugout.

The Captain, as soon as he had seen that I had matters under control, had uncharacteristically abandoned his search, in favour of finding out what had befallen his Sergeant.

Sergeant Hughes was splayed out on his back, a hole perfectly in the centre of his chest, burnt fragments of his tunic and undershirt falling into the crater that the bullet had created.

The Captain began to flap around, as he began his futile attempts to keep his long-time companion in the same mortal realm as he was.

McKay appeared, just in time to watch the Sergeant

lose consciousness, the pathetic, almost unnecessary heaves of his chest the only indication now that he was still alive. To all intents and purposes, Sergeant Nicholas Hughes was dead.

Blood began to roll from the corner of his mouth as the Captain applied some meagre pressure to the gaping hole in his breastbone. Within seconds, a similar bead was racing to the floor, emanating from one of Hughes' flared nostrils.

Hughes had seemed to tire in the last few days, as if the old-man stigma of the group had slowly started to catch up with him. Indeed, even as he lay there in an eternal rest, the wrinkles on his forehead seemed far more pronounced than they ever had done before, the bags beneath his eyes doing nothing for his otherwise youthful features.

As the weak gargles from the back of his throat began to fade away, I couldn't push the strange obsession from my mind as I watched my Sergeant die.

Now I'll never know why he was kicked out of the clergy.

I rebuked myself again for being so foolish and instead busied myself with what an NCO should do.

"McKay, check on Sargent. Make sure he's okay."

Everything had changed for me in a flash.

We had been there under instructions to be as silent as possible, as the prospect of having artillery to back us up was untenable, due to a shortage of shells.

Now though, I was preparing to move as hard and fast as I possibly could, not caring for the amount of noise that I generated, even if it was to get everyone else killed.

I had no allegiances anymore, no personal connections that would blur my vision. It was me and the enemy, each one looking exactly the same as the one that had pressed a revolver into Sergeant Hughes' breastbone, and squeezed the trigger.

There were no attachments to anything or anyone any longer.

2

Captain Arnold refused to leave the side of Sergeant Hughes for many more moments, leaving me in charge of the entire affair, something I relished but also quite quickly became petrified of.

I didn't know whether to go over and help McKay sort Bob out, or if I should stay with the Captain and offer him some sort of meagre comfort.

In the end, I opted for somewhere in the middle, trying to coax the Captain out of his trance-like state of mourning over his dead Sergeant, while also trying to ready whatever resources we had for what was to come.

In the small section of the trench I had a few things that I was absolutely certain about. For now, at least, there were no enemy soldiers posing an immediate threat. We had one man dead, another groggily coming round after being punched to the ground. Our commanding officer was otherwise indisposed, which meant that at either end of the trench, where the rest of the German army could be waiting in the wings, we were completely exposed.

At least to my left, the northernmost end of the trench, McKay was perched next to Bob, who could at the very least, offer up some sort of warning at the sign of an attack. I would need to be the one to hold the right flank, and wait for the advancing German soldiers, determined to retake their trench.

But, I would also need to drag the Captain away from Hughes, there was no time for mourning or weeping in a war such as this. Life went on. At least for a little while anyway.

"McKay," I whispered, grabbing his attention. I put one of my thumbs up. Thankfully, his went up in reply.

Bob was going to be okay, he had just been knocked unconscious and maybe lost a tooth or two, but within minutes, he would be back on his feet. McKay had managed to drag him out of the direct firing line and was now perched himself behind the wall of the dugout, revolver peering around the corner in anticipation.

I moved to the far end, to mimic his movements.

As I scurried across the wooden floorboards, I smacked the Captain on his shoulder, hard.

"Come on, Sir. Stuff to do. Leave him be."

He didn't move a muscle as I spoke to him, completely locked in one of his own little worlds that he formulated the second there was a crisis. The general advice was like that of a sleepwalker; do not disturb him, but right now, I needed my Captain to take control of the situation once more. I was beginning to flap.

As I took up position at the southern end of the trench,

my revolver bravely creeping around the corner in my right hand, my bayonet extending an inch or two further from my left, I searched myself for some element of sadness.

I had known Sergeant Hughes for months now and had ventured out with him on many an operation. And yet, I could not for the life of me find any sense of remorse at his death, nor grief. I wasn't giving myself the usual harsh treatment of searching questions and evaluations as I would normally have done.

What could I have done to save him? Was it my fault that he was dead?

I rattled the question over and over in my conscious mind, but I paid little attention to providing myself with an answer.

Hughes was a good man, a fantastic Sergeant who had nurtured me greatly in the short time that I had known him. But I hadn't quite taken to him as I had with Sergeant Needs, whose memory seemed more like a dream to me now.

I had always expected my Sergeants to have been gruff, tough men, a man who would kill everything that looked at him the wrong way. But Hughes hadn't had that about him. He was an educated man, a genteel fellow and for some reason, that had made him far less likeable. To the point where I wasn't experiencing any grief whatsoever.

The only meagre aspect of misery that I was experiencing was making me feel intensely guilty, but I could not shake it.

I will never know why he was kicked out of the clergy.
Don't be so downright stupid. Focus.
"What do you reckon, Ellis?"

The Captain began breathing heavily into my ear.

I was surprised at first that he was asking me such a question, as he always seemed so steadfast in his own decisions that he never had the need for the likes of me. But then it dawned on me the amount of quiet breaths in Hughes' ears, that had resulted in the next ingenious decision from the Captain.

Hughes was gone. I was the next confidante for the Captain.

I needed to pull myself together, and quickly, as I was still focused on Hughes' unachievable dog collar.

Not moving my gaze away from the traversing trench, I breathed out into the night, the warm air fusing with the cold in a twirling cloud.

"We're going to be flooded here, Sir. Very quickly. We're already a man down and the Boche won't take too kindly to what we've done here. Plus, we've got a matter of seconds before our guns begin to drop some shells on us here. We could move left out of the fire zone and find our own way out of the trenches further along."

The switch had been flicked, I was back in the room.

The Captain mulled over what I had said for a second or two, before replying, straight down the canal of my ear, directly into my mind.

"No. We need to head south. To the right. We have other parties further north. The artillery will be pummelling there too. I reckon no more than a hundred yards or so and then back out into No Man's Land."

"Right, Sir."

He scampered away behind me, relaying his orders to the other two, who quickly joined me where I was. The Captain seemed like he was kissing Hughes goodbye, but quickly appeared, wielding his Sergeant's revolver.

"Let's go."

He was back with us. I could take more of a back seat once again.

Bob had become far bolder than he had ever been before in recent weeks, one of the only ones to have grown as an individual since McKay's slight falter out in No Man's Land. Even so, I was surprised at the words that were breathed into the darkness, his gentle, smooth tones recently replaced by gruff, even rude noises.

"I'll go up top."

"You sure, Bob?"

"Yes, Sir. It's only a slight headache."

His curt demeanour only served to reinforce the notion that I had of Bob in recent weeks. The young, chipper lad who had been my best friend since arriving on the frontline, was now a permanently bad-tempered man, who saw nothing but ill of anyone and everyone. It was a disappointing spiral that he was in.

Even still, it had made him a better soldier, not least because he saw no issues in running an enemy soldier through with his bayonet. After all, it was their fault that we were here, according to him. In truth, I personally couldn't even recall why we were here in the first place. I had started to not care.

It was Bob who began to lead us through the deserted trenches, a common, however haunting phenomena that we had become used to each time we visited the German's side.

They much preferred to fall back, after offering up an initial weakened resistance, before swarming forwards in large numbers to repel us once more. It made no sense to them to hang around and wait for us to slaughter them.

They would be back though, and soon. Especially now that we had outstayed our welcome.

We sauntered past empty dugouts and abandoned cans of food and I noticed a distinct lack of any weapons. At least the Hun had still retained some presence of mind to take anything useful with them.

We tried to minimise as much of our collective noise as possible, the bone-dry duckboards that the Germans had laid down doing us no favours at all.

"The next fire bay, Bob," the Captain breathed as we approached another trench corner. "We'll make our way out of that one, no matter what."

I was surprised that I could hear him, his ear so close to Bob's that it was difficult to work out where one head ended and the other started. For a moment, I thought I might have even imagined what he had said.

Bob muttered nothing in reply to Captain Arnold's command, but instead tilted his head slightly, to look over his shoulder in acknowledgement.

I wondered how soon after he had done that, that Bob had realised he had made what could be one of his final moves.

The long, sneering barrel of a broom-handle pistol, a Mauser, was pressed firmly into the temple at the side of Bob's head. All it would take would be a squeeze of the trigger and Bob would be gone.

First, the skin and hair around the impact site with singe and burn, while the bullet burrowed further and further into his skull. Within moments, the barrier of the skull that was meant to protect his brain would be shattered, leaving nothing to protect poor Bob's most vital of organs.

But it wasn't the prospect of losing another of my team mates that was worrying me the most. It was the noise. The short, sharp snap of the Mauser would be all we needed to bring a tonne of bad news down on us in an instant.

The silhouetted figure that stepped out from behind the shadow of the pistol seemed confident, cocky almost. He had us exactly where he wanted us.

No one moved for what felt like an age. No one knew what was going to happen next. Neither, it seemed, did the German, even though he was the one calling all the shots.

It was Captain Arnold who moved first, apparently adamant to sign our death warrants.

It took him an awfully long time for him to finish crouching to the point where he could go no further. It was almost as if the nerves had got the better of him and he was going to ask for a little bit of privacy for a moment. But then he began to stretch his arm out.

He held Sergeant Hughes' revolver by the barrel, a demonstrative act of how subservient and peace-loving he was prepared to be. Then, locking eyes with the German as obsessively as possible, he pushed the revolver towards him, the sound of wood against metal rattling louder than a Maxim gun ever had done before.

The German eyed it suspiciously, like he half-expected it to suddenly explode in his face. But then his eyes gave him away.

That revolver would make him very popular. Very popular indeed.

It was also worth a lot of cigarettes.

The prospective glint in his eye told me everything that I needed to know about him. His fatal flaw. We all have them. He was greedy.

As the Captain gradually rose back to full height, I felt McKay lean in to me and I could feel every hair on his top lip as they swayed over the skin of my ear.

"There's a break in the wire up there, I can see it. We can get out of this fire bay here."

Like a game of Chinese whispers, I lowered my voice to so little that I was unsure if Captain Arnold would actually hear me.

"Toss the other revolver to him too. Just over to his left, just out of reach. Stay low."

Without questioning, the Captain did exactly as I had instructed, clearly with no other option in his own mind at that moment in time.

I could feel McKay breathing hard behind me, as he prepared to dart for the fire step and leap over.

The Captain repeated his motions, his arm so far outstretched that I thought he would do himself an injury if he carried on much longer. Eventually, he returned to the squatting position, ready to toss the revolver over.

It clattered to the ground perfectly, just far enough away that the German would have to stretch to reach it.

I felt a fist thump me right in the gut, as the first sounds of falling artillery only sped up our negotiations. Within seconds, the dugout would be packed with more smoke than Bob's bedroom and filled with so much dust that we would choke.

The German pressed his broom-handled pistol

further into Bob's skin and I could tell that his veins would be bulging at the news.

But he had bitten. He had taken the bait.

He began to stretch one, battered leather boot out towards the first revolver, which scraped and grinded on the wood as it found its way to him.

The second proved more problematic though. It was too far for him, he would have to alleviate some of the pressure on Bob's head. But his greed was the only justification that he needed and so his leg continued to manoeuvre towards the revolver.

It was too much for him and his attempts at rebalancing himself were futile. He staggered over to his left, just an inch or two, but just enough for what I needed him for.

I raised my Webley up to my eye, so that my arm was leaning over the top of Captain Arnold's head.

I suddenly realised that my hand was quivering terribly, and I was finding it difficult to distinguish where the German's chest was.

I blamed it on the artillery for a moment, the ground tremoring shakes offering me no assistance in the slightest.

But I knew what it really was, I couldn't shake the thought from my head.

I really need a sip of that paraffin. Just to steady myself.

I needed to take my opportunity now, the German was already remedying his mistake.

I squeezed the trigger, as hard as I could.

Bang.

Bob suddenly spun away from the German, smacking

into him as he collapsed to the ground, opening up the German's figure for me to aim at.

Bang. Bang. Bang.

The German slumped to the floor with a thud. None of us watched over him to see if he was going to be getting up again.

Instead, we fell back on the ancient military tactic that had got soldiers out of trouble for centuries.

We ran away.

3

I was particularly glad to make it back to the *Café de Fleurs* that night.

As ever, everything had seemed to blur into a distant memory, one that would only come back in my dreams in the coming weeks.

It hadn't been our most successful raid, that much was certain. With one man wounded and another dead it was, in fact, one of the worst raids that I had been on since I had started on them.

Progressively, over the last few weeks, the human cost of conducting such raids had spiked, not just with our team, but all the others too.

The Germans were slowly becoming more astute as to ways of repelling us or inflicting heavier casualties. Booby-traps were now common place, as was the hand-to-hand fighting that they had been so keen to avoid before.

Maybe it was also something to do with the fact that there wasn't really too much variation to our role, we always did the same thing.

Jump in, kill and injure, ransack, then leave. We never got any further than the fire bays themselves. We would need to change it up a bit eventually.

The raids had become less effective too, especially in the way of intelligence gathering. To begin with, it wasn't too difficult to locate a map or a communiqué or two, as they were frequently left lying about. Now, it was just as easy to find them, but perhaps too easy.

It was so easy in fact, that I wasn't really sure why we were still out there, as almost all of it was falsified or made up in some way. There was no real option of acting upon any of the intelligence that we gained.

Maybe that was why the only place where I seemed capable of any kind of happiness was back at the café. In the past, I had gleaned small droplets of glee and delight at the amount of information that we had come back with, or the calibre of prisoner that we had taken.

Now, none of it seemed to matter. We were losing men like Sergeant Hughes for no reason whatsoever. We were increasingly morphing into the new infantry.

The café had become the only image that I had that resembled something of a safe haven. I could barely remember home, the world that I was in being so far removed from the premise of one that it felt like it had all been a figment of my imagination.

I dreamed of the café, both day and night; when I was both there and absent from it. It had become one of the very few things in my life that I actually cared about.

"Paul!" I bellowed as I entered the small, but adequate café. It was far too small for what was being demanded of it, but the owner was more than happy to let as many men stack themselves in, to help them forget the war for an hour or two.

"Monsieur Ellis! It is good to see you back in one piece again!"

He was a pleasant fellow, who spoke excellent English, which was just as well owing to the number of us who descended on his establishment day after day. He was accommodating too, sacrificing the top floor of his building plus two other rooms below for us to use as our home.

Paul Sancy, and the rest of his family, were squeezed into two tiny rooms along the corridor from our own, a small sacrifice, he had said, for the men who came to his country's assistance.

"It is good to see you too! You tubby little fellow!"

He bellowed uproariously each and every time that I had said it, and I wondered frequently if he would have had the same reaction, if someone was to enlighten him as to what I was calling him. Deep down, I think he knew.

"My old soak! Back again!" he squeezed out in between chuckles. That phrase, he did know the true meaning of, as McKay had been so quick to enlighten him.

"Speaking of which, where is my drink?" I winked at him.

Paul had become my main provider of the paraffin that I now needed to keep on going, especially now that Earnshaw was holed up in some hospital somewhere and unable to top me up. It was no trouble for Paul to source me the paraffin, especially at the price that I was paying for its provision anyway.

"Coming, my friend. Coming!"

It had started out as a little bit of a joke, a quick top up of the paraffin-like liquid in my bloodstream immediately after a raid. But slowly, it had become a desire of mine, a superstition, one or two may have even said a necessity.

They may have been right, to a degree, the quivering in my hand that I had experienced as I pointed the Webley towards Bob had refused to subside. I was a slave to it, hiding my right hand in my trouser pocket all the way back to the café, where Paul's routine remedy would sort it out.

"Andrew," breathed Paul into my face as he bent down to pour me a cup of his terrible cognac, "where is Nicholas?"

He said it in such a way that I thought he was deliberately trying to rile me, every syllable becoming an exhalation of breath and an odious one at that.

I recoiled slightly from him, the Frenchman mistaking my tears of discomfort for ones of sadness.

It was the first time since Hughes had died that I felt any kind of distress at his passing, and not just because I wouldn't get to ask him my burning question about the clergy.

He was not just a good soldier, but an upstanding and loyal member of the human race and now, in the blink of an eye, he was just a memory.

He had been the one who was the most experienced out of all of us, the eldest in the group that we could all look to for guidance. In a group of brothers, he had been our father.

Now that he was gone, our little team would never be the same.

The Frenchman had noticed the changed expression on my face, from one that usually exuded confidence and buoyancy, to one that was now dejected and scared. I was more like the boy soldier that I had been the year before.

As if he needed to hear the words from my mouth, he waited, bottle in hand awaiting my response.

"Erm…He's…He's gone, Paul. He won't be coming back."

I gulped at the cognac and let the glass clatter to the table loudly.

He thought for a moment, before refilling my glass.

"That is a shame, Andrew. He was a nice man. A good man. He was always very kind and gentle. He used to pray with my children before bed time."

"Did he? I didn't know that."

"Oh, yes. Every night since you came here. He was a gentle man, he always liked talking to my children. I think they reminded him of his own."

He registered the look on my face.

"You did not know he had children?"

I clearly didn't know him as well as I had thought.

"No…"

"Three. All boys."

"Right."

"He had seemed slower more recently though. Reluctant to pray with them it seemed. He looked tired. More exhausted. Like all of you really. Something had happened in the last few weeks."

It was a probing statement, but one that did not necessitate an answer, which I did not give him the pleasure of having. Paul was not a nosy man, but the human desire for knowledge had overwhelmed him on that one.

"Anyway, I will leave you now, Andrew. I am sorry to hear about Nicholas. But this is war."

He had learnt the harrowing lesson of this war. Don't get attached to someone too easily, they'll only break your heart.

I watched him as he scurried back behind the counter, whispering to his wife about the latest demise of one of their cohabitants. She looked over at me with forlorn little eyes and the kind of withering sympathetic look that is given to a child on news of their parent's death.

I nodded towards her, with a weak smile on my face in thanks of her compassion and raised my glass to her gently.

"What you doin', you big pansy?"

His drink hit the table first, then his fist as he slid his buttocks into the battered wooden chair next to mine.

"Just told Porky Paul about Sergeant Hughes."

"Oh…Right…What does he actually care?"

"What?"

"Him…He doesn't really care for Hughes, does he? That's just one less person to pay for these dreadful drinks."

"I think you've probably had enough of them tonight."

"You're a fine one to talk, Ellis."

A passer-by to our conversation may have mistaken it for something far more malicious than it was. But, in actual fact, this was why both McKay and I had grown so incredibly close in recent weeks.

We were both able to acknowledge our weaknesses in one another's company and, in doing so, joke about them.

It made us better people, helped us to realise that we weren't perfect and that if we didn't improve on them, we would die.

We had bonded in recent weeks, over a smoke and a packet of playing cards, as he slowly tried to rediscover his feet after what had happened out in No Man's Land. It was still not referred to by any that knew of it, not even after a skinful of drinks or an emotionally charged argument. It went unsaid.

"I liked Hughes. He was good to me," he said, lifting his glass towards Paul to come and refill it. I knew that he would be marking down how much he was putting in our glasses before he had even topped it up. He would want to be paid.

"Me too."

"He always trusted me. Always believed in me."

Paul scurried away, hopping over extended legs and bashing into tables.

"He died for me," he suddenly blurted.

"How do you mean?"

I wondered for a moment what was going through McKay's head. He was trying so desperately to prove to us that he was still worth being part of the team but to do what he had done, to get to the point of actually stealing intelligence, he must have had a genuine belief that he would end the war.

In my view, it wasn't treason that had made him do it, but downright stupidity. I knew that I could trust him, but I wasn't sure that I could fall back on his intellect.

"If Hughes hadn't got in the way. That bullet would have been for me."

"That's just the way that it goes. Besides, if Hughes hadn't got in the way, that German would have been in the dugout with the Captain and me. So, Hughes saved all of us. There was nothing any of us could have done, Fritz."

His nickname still clung to him like a bad odour, despite the fact that it had begun to lose its meaning. At first, it was because of his hatred of all men of English heritage, particularly those of the aristocracy.

But now, he defended the Captain with every fibre of his being, something I drew out of him for my own entertainment. But he had also taken to me, something which I had not quite been expecting. It was inevitable that we should have become friends however, our unnatural enjoyment and obsession with going over the top would only serve to make us stronger companions.

We had a moment in contemplative silence, before he leant over and started rummaging around in his trouser pockets.

He slapped the playing cards down on the surface of the table triumphantly, with a broad grin sweeping over his bruised face.

I looked at his hand that had placed the cards down and saw that they too, were blackened and bruised by the constant fighting that we put our bodies through. His knuckles were ripped and torn as if he had stuck his hand in a threshing machine.

He was still a hard fighter, made harder still by the notion that he had to make amends for what he had done before. The bruises and scratches had become as much a part of him as his gravelly Scottish tones and I couldn't picture him without them any longer.

"Cigarette, Fritz?" I asked as I teased the packet right under his nose. I knew that he wouldn't say no.

"Go on then."

"While you deal those out," I lit his cigarette for him, "finish telling me that story about your father and the fat Earl. I was enjoying that."

"Oh yeah. Now…Where did I get to on that one?"

Sergeant Hughes was dead. But life carried on as normal for us. It had to.

4

"Right then. Does anyone have any questions or observations that they wish to bring up?"

The debriefing had seemed like it had far surpassed the length of any others that I had ever experienced, but even after all this time, Captain Arnold still seemed adamant on making it last just a little bit longer.

"Nothing? Okay. I have one final thing to ask. Andrew, how is Bob?"

I looked up from my semi-dozing, startled. I hadn't been expecting a question like that one to be thrown on me this late in the game, especially one I did not have an answer for.

I knew that Bob wasn't dead, but in a hospital bed somewhere way behind the lines, relatively safe. But past that, I hadn't really given him too much thought. It could almost be taken for a lack of consideration for my former comrade.

"Not really sure, Sir."

"But aren't you two—"

"I've been to see him, Sir," interrupted McKay, ignoring my glares from across the room. He hadn't done anything wrong, but I had learnt from experience that if he was to go around sneaking off on his own, then the outcome would not be good.

"And?"

"He's okay, Sir. He'll survive anyway. Just a slight graze to his side. Could have been a lot worse by all accounts."

"Well, thank goodness for that. Any idea of when we might expect him back?"

"A day or two, Sir. Doctors reckoned much longer than that, but he's a stubborn old fool. Didn't want to miss out on any of the fun."

I was glad that he was going to be okay, but I was more thrilled for the rest of the team that he was insisting on coming back so soon. Lance Corporal Bob Sargent was the likeable one in our team, the NCO who seemed to care about the rest of his men.

That wasn't to say that I didn't care, but he chose to show it a lot more than me and it had begun to grind on me of late.

"Good. Good. Well, it will do us all a favour when he's back. Isn't that right, Andrew?"

He was goading me, but I knew I just had to accept it.

"Yes, Sir."

"Right then, chaps. In the light of everything that has happened, the brass have decided to call off all our training for today. There will be no need to pack your things for that little excursion we were going to take."

"We're having a break?" I wondered if the other two could sense the pure jubilation in my voice. They must have done.

"Of sorts," teased Captain Arnold.

The training that we had been subjected to in recent weeks was utterly torturous for the likes of us. It seemed completely meaningless to continue with standard infantryman training; bayonet practice, rifle firing and trench clearing tactics.

We didn't use bayonets in the conventional sense, we didn't take rifles with us and we were the ones who had devised the clearing tactics. It was senseless to force us to listen to someone else give the lectures like they had been there themselves.

Nevertheless, it had led to healthy competition between all of us. I may have been a terrible shot with a revolver, but with a Lee-Enfield rifle, I was the best out of the bunch. I was a crack shot.

"Of sorts," queried McKay, "what's that supposed to mean?"

The Captain stared us both down for a few moments, as if his command of just two men were not worthy of such an officer as he.

"We've got a briefing instead."

"Another one?" I blurted, which was met by the huge palm of Captain Arnold.

"Yes."

"But there's only three of us!"

"I don't think that really matters this time. I've been hearing rumours."

He looked about the room, as if a horde of Germans were waiting right outside the door to hear what he had to say.

"My chums up at HQ. They've been feeding me some information about upcoming operations."

"What kind of operations?" I asked, tentatively.

"To be honest, I'm not sure. They're not sure, in fact."

"Then how does that actually help us in the slightest?"

The Captain cleared his throat, as if what he was about to tell us would only come from his mouth once, and we simply had to hear it the first time.

"They think that some sort of operation is about to begin. They think it is an experimental type of undertaking that hasn't properly been utilised before. I reckon it's big. Bigger than anything that I've been in before. There's a lot of different men involved."

"How can you be sure?"

"There's more Majors up there right now than one of Bach's compositions. Trust me, it's big."

I failed to see how a team of just three men, which we were for the time being, would be able to make that much of an impact in this kind of operation.

"Sir, how are we going to help? Surely the three of us would just be better off sitting this one out? We'll just be in the way."

"Nice try, Ellis. But I don't think we're going to have to worry about numbers. I'm sure they'll be bolstering us up in preparation for this one."

"Besides," interrupted McKay, "Bob will be back in a day or two. So, will Earnshaw."

"I won't hold my breath on that one," I chuckled.

The meeting was adjourned the minute the Captain arose from his chair, and we began our daily ritual of heading downstairs to have a chat with Porky Paul, the café owner.

As our boots thudded disturbingly loudly on the

staircase, I began to recall the sheer numbers of men that I had seen in the last few weeks, that had no consequence to me until now.

They had seemed like a rag-tag bunch of men, with very little or no discipline, getting themselves involved in fights and prostitution as if they had no inhibitions whatsoever.

It had struck me as odd, particularly when a lot of them had seemed far older than the average Tommy, who would look old if he managed to make it to the age of twenty-five.

These men were in their thirties at the very youngest, but old enough to know when to throw a punch or to simply take a jibe on the chin. These men were unruly and so ill-disciplined that I wondered whether or not they actually had any officers.

It was almost as if the army had become so desperate that they had chucked a khaki suit towards a group of vagabonds, and shipped them to France. They were rogues.

The lack of discipline was of no real consequence to me and did not trouble me in the slightest, I wasn't being asked to bring them into line after all. It just struck me as odd, that these old, unruly men, were even here in the first place, as they seemed like the kind of men that would rather go to where they could get the most beer, and this close to the frontline certainly wasn't it.

They were here for a reason. Someone had told them to be here.

5

In groups of five to ten men, we began to stumble and fall into the briefing room that we had frequented so many times before. But this time was different for me, it was different for McKay. We weren't going in as part of a wider group that we could call our family, this time we were just a pair. It was just the two of us.

We sat down in our usual seats, near enough to the front so that we could see and hear, but not quite in the front row where we could get picked on.

The first thing that I noticed about the room was that there was a Major sat up near the front, with all the other officers sitting alongside him, who seemed as pleased as anything to be sat near him. I for one didn't have a clue who he was.

"Who's that then?"

McKay didn't know either.

"One of Bach's scales, I'd imagine," I chuckled.

"Eh?"

I didn't have time to explain the joke to McKay, and I

wasn't sure he'd get it even if I did, as Major Grant, the man who kicked off all our briefings, stood up. He called the room to a hush.

"Gentlemen. You may be wondering why you are gathered here in such large numbers and under such secrecy. I won't beat around the bush but get straight to the point."

"That makes a change," muttered McKay under his breath.

"You may have heard about the large offensive in Ypres last month. Some of you may have even heard about the way the attack took place. It is with this in mind that I would like to brief you on an operation that we would like you all to be a part of."

I had indeed heard about the offensive from the month previous, but I wasn't entirely sure what to make of it. At first, it seemed completely unbelievable, but the numbers of men discussing it told me it had to be true.

I had taken it all with a pinch of salt, as you could never be too certain what was gospel and what was gossip when the conveyors were war-weary soldiers.

"The Major here," he nodded towards the esteemed guest among us, "commands one of the newly-formed tunnelling companies in the Royal Engineers. It was his men that dug the tunnel beneath Hill 60 last month."

The Major barely even flinched at his mention, not taking his enduring gaze off Grant for a moment. I wondered if he was even listening.

Regardless, it certified that the rumours that had been muttered throughout the towns and villages had, in fact, been true.

Someone, somewhere, had been digging tunnels and then blowing them up.

I tried not to delve into the moral and ethical arguments for such a method of war as, until now at least, they had not affected my war or my experience of it.

The draw was too deep however, and I zoned out from Major Grant's monotonous tones for a moment, as I began to draw upon a conclusion.

Men had been killing each other for centuries and it was only natural that a progression should be made in the methods of doing so.

Although, I couldn't quite see where the digging and blowing up of tunnels was really relevant to me and my war.

Focus back in and you might just find out.

"The Major's men have been working exceptionally hard in the last couple of months in this part of the line. You may have noticed some of them out and about around here, but they do, for the most part live under the ground. The Major informs me that they frequently won't see sky for at least a week at a time."

I was struggling to see where this was all going, but the longer the preamble, the longer I had to become concerned.

"You chaps might be wondering where you all fit into this. I am here to enlighten you. It all fits, gentlemen, into a wider cooperative effort between numerous different companies and across a wide front."

A blackboard that had been waiting ever so patiently behind him was suddenly rotated, to reveal to us a map of the area, like we had been treated to on so many other occasions. But this one was different to the others.

Invisible Frontline

This map managed to draw gasps and questioning groans as men pulled themselves forwards in their seats to get a proper look.

"Well, stone me," muttered McKay, as if the map held the key to every question that we had.

The map wasn't normal, in the sense that it didn't cover what we had expected it to.

Normally, a map such as this one would start with the British frontline at the bottom, No Man's Land just above that and then the German frontline right at the very top, where it was easy for everyone to see.

But the bottom of this map only just touched on the German frontline, the rest of the blackboard was taken up with the squiggling and intertwining lines of the German reserve lines, their communication trenches and their artillery pieces.

This map, instead of covering the few hundred yards between one frontline and the other, covered miles. It must have done.

The murmurs slowly began to die down as one by one the men in the room, the officers included, realised that we were looking at a detailed map behind the Germans' lines.

The more that I stared at the map, the more I began to feel the pessimism begin to surge from the deepest pit of my bowels and into the back of my throat.

Things were not looking promising in the slightest.

6

"I'm still not entirely sure why they think that we want to die so much," muttered McKay as we stood over a smaller map than the one in the briefing room.

We had been given a more detailed map that focused in on the area of interest for what we had been asked to do.

Bob had walked away from the hospital while we were out at the briefing and so the four of us; Captain Arnold, Bob, McKay and me, had been studying the table top in a near-perfect silence for the best part of an hour now. The longer we looked at it, the more unbelievable the whole scheme seemed.

"So, boss," McKay continued, "let me get this straight."

He shuffled the map around on the table top slightly, so we all got a better view of where he was pointing.

"We enter the line here," he tapped the map, "like any other raid."

Captain Arnold took his pencil from his top pocket and circled where McKay's finger had been, "Correct."

"Then what? I get they want us to go through the communication dugouts and into the support lines, but...how?"

"What do you mean?"

"I think he means, how do they actually expect us to survive, Sir? How are several small groups going to push through several hundreds of Germans, all sitting in their trenches waiting for us?"

My hand was quivering as I spoke, so it was quickly hidden in the depths of my pocket. Bob, who had remained uncharacteristically quiet since he returned, gave me a slight sideways glance, the kind that told me he had already spotted what I was trying to hide.

"Well, we'll have artillery to force them underground."

"Everyone in the artillery seems to be cross-eyed, Sir."

Arnold looked across at McKay for some sort of elaboration.

"They always miss, Sir. It never works."

"It will this time. They've had plenty of practice. Trust me, it's all quite simple really."

We spent the next half an hour going through the plan, the one that was being forced upon us and would likely be getting us killed.

In a few days' time we would cross No Man's Land, enter the German line, then push deeper into their lines before leaving their trenches. From there, if there was any of us left, we would journey about six miles, towards a supply dump, which we would proceed to destroy.

There was just the small task of making it back to see

to after that. I wasn't hopeful, in fact, I was convinced that someone truly despised me and had been sitting in their quarters somewhere, thinking of the most ridiculous plan that would see me killed.

At least we wouldn't have to do any of that awful training for the next couple of days. Instead, we would be studying the maps, over and over, until we were dreaming about which route to take and where everything was.

The only issue being, we only had experience of their fire bays, anything further back than that and the whole of the British forces were blind, not just us.

The whole affair was made more uncomfortable by the fact that I now had an additional stripe stitched into my arm. The Sergeant stripes had been handed to me by Captain Arnold as we had left the briefing room, under the strictest instructions that I was to have them sewn on immediately.

I was Sergeant Ellis now, and I should demand to be addressed as such.

For a while, I felt odd, which at first, I mistook for guilt. After all, I was effectively wearing a dead man's jacket. There wouldn't have been a chance of the extra stripe had Hughes still been alive.

But then, I realised that I felt no guilt at all, I still felt no remorse over Sergeant Hughes' death. Not in the same way that I had lamented the death of Sergeant Needs anyway.

I didn't even feel slightly guilty at the prospect of having to tell McKay the news either. He was now the most experienced raider that we had in our little group, so by rights, he should have been the one to take the promotion.

But he was weaker than me, more fragile. In recent weeks I had become more robust, resistant even and that had made me a better soldier, even if it had made me a worse man.

Captain Arnold disappeared from the room momentarily, while Bob lay on his bunk staring at the ceiling. So, for a while I stood, just with McKay, overlooking the map.

"Ciggy?"

He took one and we both stood in silence as we took our first few drags.

"This one's going to get us killed, isn't it, Andrew?"

"Probably. I bet I can last longer than you though."

He chuckled weakly, out of a sad realisation of reality.

"Do you reckon they've allowed for enough time? I mean we've got nearly seven miles to cover. And it's not exactly going to be a nice flat field is it? There might even be some people who want to kill us."

"I'm sure they have, Fritz. The brass hats want us to succeed, don't they? They will have definitely gone over it a few times since it was drawn up. The tunnellers have been going for months, this hasn't been a spur of the moment type thing."

"I suppose you're right."

"I usually am."

I was trying to reassure him, but I needed to hear it coming from my own mouth, just as much as he did. It seemed like suicide, downright stupidity, to try and cover a distance so big, in such a short space of time.

It wouldn't surprise me if we still found ourselves sausage side by the time the sun came up.

"It's a simple enough plan, Fritz. They're always the

best ones. It'll be easy enough. We just have to keep our minds in it."

I tried to remain as coy as possible, but he knew full well what I was referring to. It wasn't that I didn't trust him to get the job done, but I was concerned about where his head was. Physically, he would kill anyone that tried to come at him, but he still needed the mental awareness of what he was doing and why.

We simply could not have a repeat of what had happened before.

"We'll see it through, McKay."

Bob suddenly scoffed from the other side of the room, hoisting himself up to sit at the end of his bed.

"Will you?"

"What's that supposed to mean?"

"We always saw it through together, Andrew. You shot me the other night, if you'd forgotten!"

"You know I hadn't."

"Forgotten, or seen it through together?"

"Oh, be quiet."

Bob's permanent bad temper, and my constant exhaustion, had led to a fiery furnace that burned away under the surface for many weeks now. It was difficult to talk to him or see eye to eye, which made the memories that we had together far more painful.

He had been the one who had taken me under his wing when I had first arrived in France and now, we seemed constantly at one another's throats.

"Maybe my family were right. You know, Andrew, they always wanted me to join the Navy, follow in my ancestors' footsteps and all that. I'm beginning to regret going against their wishes now. You see, if I had joined the Navy then I wouldn't have ended up in the same room as a drunk and a traitor!"

I normally tried not to bite, but this time, I saw red.

"You leave him out of this!" I bellowed at the top of my lungs, McKay genuinely shocked at the sudden escalation. "If you have a problem with me, that's fine, but you know the agreement!"

"I do have a problem with you! You're a drunk and a liability, look at the state of you!"

He waved his arms up and down as he rose from his bed, like he was offering me up for sale on a street corner.

"If you have a problem with me, why don't you take it up with the Captain?"

"I wish I could! But I know that wouldn't get me anywhere whatsoever! He has your back more than any other moron here!"

"If it's such a big problem to you, why has no one ever mentioned it before?"

"They're scared of you! Why can't you see it? This is what happens when someone brings it up, you get defensive!"

I knew he was right, but there was something raging from the very pit of my stomach that made me want to carry on, I was enjoying this too much.

"If you don't think Arnold would sort it for you, why not go higher up? If you're convinced that it's such a big problem, when men are being killed every single second, go and find a Major or a General who is going to look at it for more than fifteen seconds!"

"Maybe I will!" he screamed, spit and saliva soaking the floorboards at his feet. Momentarily, I glanced over at McKay, as if looking to him for some back up might come in handy at some point soon. His head was down, staring hard at the map as if nothing else was going on around him.

"You've changed Andrew. Do you not remember how you were? You were scared. You froze. But now you've forgotten how you started out. You used to care for everyone. Now you care for nothing but that hip flask! That's become more important than your mates. You haven't even given Hughes a second thought, have you?"

He prodded his index finger into my chest, where he knew full well he would feel the solid resistance of the hip flask.

"That is not true!" I lied, pushing him away from me in disgust, but somehow thinking I managed to convince him. I had thought about Hughes and the way in which he died, but I had felt no genuine, long-lasting pangs of remorse for his death. Even when Paul had told me that he had three young sons. There was nothing.

"You give no one any thought or consideration. You care more for what you are able to bring back and show off than who you bring back!"

He was pointing accusingly at the German imperial flag that was now wrapped around the pillow on my bed, the gentle mustiness being the very thing that I had needed to send me off to sleep each and every night.

I was losing the argument badly and desperately needed to move the conversation on, away from me.

"You've changed too, Bob. You were kind, gentle. Now look at you. You're just as aggressive and defensive as me! You're only like this because a girl left you, don't you realise there are bigger things at stake here than women!"

It was probably one step too far. It had only happened three or four days ago. Still too raw.

She had found someone else, someone that wasn't at war and who might actually still be alive by the time she wrote her next letter. Everything had changed for him after that. There was no more kissing of the ring finger when he was nervous, no more kind and caring persona. He had just become an empty shell.

A man waiting to die.

"I'm sorry. Bob..." I tried to catch his eye, "I'm sorry."

It was too late; the damage was already irreparable. The cracks had deepened considerably.

If there had been anywhere to go, I was sure that Bob would have stormed out from the room, but there was nowhere. He also seemed to be in a considerable pain, as he carefully lowered himself back onto his bunk, clutching at his side.

I knew that every word that he had breathed had been right. And I knew that McKay felt exactly the same way.

I was drinking far too much of the burning liquid at every opportunity that I could find. In fact, I had needed a sip when Bob had started his tirade, but thought better of going for the flask in fear of reinforcing his point.

My hand was still shaking uncontrollably, and I was having a great fight with it in my pocket, trying to keep it as steady as possible.

I knew that everyone else around had more than likely seen and taken note of it, including the Captain at some point. But, for some reason, the loyalty to one another in this group meant that it all went unsaid, until an eruption like Bob's.

I knew that I could still trust him, however. This was the kind of group that could scream obscenities in each other's faces, but the minute an outsider spoke ill of me, they would all have my back.

Something needed to be done about the situation however and as Sergeant, it fell to me to implement a course of action.

As far as I was concerned, what I did when we were behind the lines was of no real consequence, as long as I could still perform when I was called to do so. To me, I still believed that I was executing all of my duties to the very best of my abilities.

The only way to relieve the tension in the team, would be to remove Bob.

I would talk to the Captain about it after this little jolly that we had planned.

7

"Ay up, anyone miss me?"

Harry Earnshaw appeared in the doorway, looking as fresh as if he had just arrived from the latest boatload of recruits from England.

There was something about him though, that was ever so slightly different to the way that he normally looked. He was still tall and stick thin, which he had always been, but there was an air about him that made him feel a bit bedraggled.

The bags that clutched at the underside of our eyes were not present on Harry, but he had tiny little red veins running right the way across the surface of his eyeballs. It looked as though he hadn't been to bed in days.

It was good to have him back though, not like anyone really showed it, however.

"No, not me," I replied, giving him a slap on the back.

"It was certainly a lot quieter without you around, Harry."

"I'll take that as a compliment, Sir."

"You really shouldn't."

"Oh, well I'm really glad I came back. You lot are charming."

"How long's it been, Harry? Two months? Did you have a nice break then?"

"Leave off will ya? I got hit in the stomach, that's the worse place to get hit. I couldn't eat for weeks! And it was only six weeks, alright? There were complications. I got some sort of an infection."

"Must have been a pretty serious one for you to miss all the action," Bob mockingly joked, speaking for the first time since our little bout.

"It was serious. They told me that I actually nearly died."

"Funny that," chimed in McKay as he flicked a cigarette into his mouth, "'cos so did we."

There was a healthy dose of laughter for a moment or two, even Captain Arnold joined in. It did us all wonders to have him back, as we hadn't had any kind of positive news in what felt like months. We all needed a little respite from it all.

"I forgot you lot were all comedians...Thanks for coming to visit me by the way," he added sarcastically, which sent us off into another round of chuckling.

"Didn't want to catch anything, especially that bad luck that you seem to attract," McKay was beginning to enjoy himself, his little face lighting up with every phrase that drew a laugh.

Earnshaw didn't waste another moment, "Right, well, if you lot are going to continue to be horrible to me, then I won't hand out the gifts that I managed to scavenge for you."

"Did that infection leave you with a sensitive side, Earnshaw?"

"So, what if it did? Do you want these presents, or not?"

We all bundled around him, like he was selling the most impressive conkers the schoolyard had ever seen.

He began rummaging around in the coarse sack that he had plonked at his feet, "Alright, alright, give a man some space. Come on, back off."

He went into his best street entertainer routine, bringing a smile to all of our faces before he had even produced the gifts.

"For Lance Corporal Bob Sargent, the man who only ever stops smoking to sleep, a carton of the finest French cigarettes."

Bob took them gratefully, before immediately delving into them to try them out.

"For McKay, the boy who never got to grow up, some barley sugars for your sweet tooth."

"Cheers, Harry."

He proceeded to produce a nice leather-bound notebook for the Captain, to write down all those thoughts that he had in his head, before turning to me.

"And for you, Andrew. I got this," he pulled a bottle from his bag, the dark, thick liquid within just sloshing around gently in the void. "What?" he said, observing the look on my face, "you still drink the stuff, right?"

"Oh yeah, absolutely. It's just...Oh never mind," I said hurriedly, grabbing the bottle, "Thanks, Harry."

I concealed the bottle quickly, aware that before long Bob's eyes would be on it, causing some unnecessary tension. Besides, I didn't want anyone else to take a single drop of it.

"Anyone going to fill me in then, or what?"

"You've been gone so long we'll be here all year, mate."

"Very good. Come on though, update me."

No one seemed willing to take the lead; the Captain was already locked in his mind once again, dallying on his new notebook, Bob was too busy making his way through all his cigarettes, while McKay just seemed totally averse to joining in.

I started to fill him in on all the comings and goings of recent weeks; how many times we had been out and even how one of the other raiding parties came back with as many prisoners as they had men. He seemed to like that one.

I informed him about what we spent our days doing and the gossip from the café, that carried on hustling and bustling below our feet. But I was just dancing around the inevitable news that he wanted.

"The chap who came in to fill your boots bought it on his second time out."

"That's a shame."

"Should have been you."

"I know."

He must have known by now, he had been here for nearly two hours so he must have noticed the change in dynamic. He was just waiting for the words to come from my mouth.

"Two Pews got put in the ground."

I felt sick as I said it, the two of them had been quite close.

"So I heard."

"Who from?"

"Some orderly in the hospital, kept me posted on as much as he could. Contrary to popular belief, I actually like you lot. That's a blow about Hughes though."

"Yeah."

"That orderly also told me though that you shot young Bob over there, so I wasn't really sure what he was saying was true or a lie."

I looked at him, my expression unchanged.

"You did shoot...Why? What did he do? Bad mouth your mother or something?"

He was the only one to find his joke even mildly amusing.

"It's a long story."

We were thankfully interrupted by a reluctant shadow standing in the doorway. Stepping forward, his face was brought into the light a little bit more.

He was mid-twenties, had to be, so older than me and most of the others in the room, but somehow, he looked far younger. Maybe it had something to do with the fact that his face was clean and unblemished.

That wasn't to say that ours were dirty, but what we had seen and been through gave a face a sort of grime over the surface of it, the kind of grime that will never come off a man fully. In good time, I was sure this young lad would have his own helping of permanent dirt over his face.

"You alright, mate? You lost?"

He seemed reluctant to speak at first, but when he did his voice was clear and confident.

"I am looking for Captain Terence Arnold?"

"He's not here at the moment, want us to pass on a message?"

The lad shook his head. Earnshaw was having the same thoughts as I was.

"You from HQ?"

The young lad looked puzzled for a moment, but still refused to speak. His head was an odd shape, almost square like and his tiny ratty eyes were set back from the rest of his face, making his nose seem to protrude even further than it actually did.

"Then why are you here?" I eventually managed to spit out.

"I'm Private David Hamilton. I was told to report to Captain Arnold here. I am a replacement for his team."

We all exchanged looks with one another for a moment, concerned. We didn't like outsiders all that much, especially posh ones.

"You're a private? Has your father disowned you or something?"

"Is he one of your father's customers, McKay?" I coughed across the room, laughing at my joke before I'd even managed to utter it.

"You had better come in then, son. We are the rest of Captain Arnold's section."

"You can have that bed over there, Hamilton. That's the spare one now."

He made his way over to his new bed and chucked his kit down next to it.

"No one else going to bother showing him around then?" muttered Earnshaw as he hauled himself to his feet with a grunt. "Pathetic. The lot of you."

"Oi, button it. You've had six weeks off remember."

Earnshaw began showing Hamilton around the room and giving initial introductions, in much the same way that he had done with me when I had first arrived.

"So, have you met the Captain yet?"

"No, why do you ask?"

"Just thought you might be a family friend, that's all. And this is Corporal And…Oh sorry Andrew. Didn't realise you had another stripe now. This is Sergeant Ellis. I guess that makes him the one that's in charge at the moment."

That was the moment that I could pinpoint the weight on my shoulders becoming even heavier. I had not thought the responsibility through before, but now I had a new soldier in our midst, and it would be my responsibility to nurture and train him. And I was struggling to maintain a simple friendship with Bob, never mind thinking about Hamilton as well.

8
———

As Earnshaw, McKay and I made our way towards the dugouts, I tried to remember the last time that I had been down one.

I supposed that it had been many months before now, when I was still regarded as a frontline soldier, when I had been granted the rare opportunity of heading underground to try and get some rest.

It was an odd experience, that much I could recall, the entire time spent in fear for my life that the next earth tremor would signal the collapse of the underground bunker that we were in, to be buried alive.

When I had last been down there, it had been a simple enough structure; one long, underground corridor with three entry points so we didn't suffocate to death, with beds aligning the walls on either side, where exhausted soldiers could get their heads down.

Once mine had hit the canvas of the bunk bed, I was out like a light, which was probably just as well, as I didn't think my nerves would have lived up to the test of being underground for too long. I didn't know how the Major's tunnellers could go weeks at a time without feeling fresh air. Even if it was the smoke infested, cordite filled air of the Western Front.

It was the men that we would meet down there that were the source of my curiosity. I wanted to see exactly who it was that we were going to be putting our trust in once everything had kicked off and got underway.

I needed to be able to trust them more than I could trust myself.

"You ever been down one of these before?"

"Once or twice. Just to get some sleep. A while ago now and nothing like what they're trying to achieve now...This is it over here."

The entrance to the rabbit warren was unsuspecting and inconspicuous, a simple wooden doorframe leaning into a mound of mud was all that was apparent above the surface.

As we moved through the small wooden doorway, we came to the top of a rather steep gradient, adorned quite expertly with wooden beams used for the staircase that zig-zagged their way down to the base of the complex.

Above our heads, a hand painted sign, seemingly done by a child, advertised the name of the bunker that we were now entering.

The Rat Run.

We continued down the stairs in silence, as I took the time to test the structure around me, by slapping the great steel beams that held up the clay and mud above our heads. I wondered how many railways back in Britain were now unserviceable due to the amount of material commandeered for projects such as these.

Despite my apprehension, the structure that we found ourselves in was of a remarkable integrity and quality. So much so, that I began to question why anyone would still be on the surface, apart from a few sentries, when comparative safety was just a forty-foot descent below them.

"Alright lads," called a voice from a landing area on the stairs.

As we descended closer to him, I realised that he was stripped to his waist and had been smoking for many hours now, the cigarette ends piling up around his boots, which appeared to be nothing more than a pair of wellingtons trimmed down to his ankles.

"We're looking for the tunnellers?"

"Yeah…It won't be hard to find us. We're the only ones down here." He stared us out for a minute. "Got a light?" he suddenly piped up and McKay was only too happy to help.

"Ran out of matches about an hour ago. Can't leave my post see."

"And what is it you're actually here for?"

"Gas. When the gas comes a-creeping, I go a-screeching…Anyway, don't let me keep ya, you were obviously going somewhere. Straight down there to the gallery chaps."

"Why's he giving us directions? It's not difficult to get lost down here," muttered Earnshaw moodily once the sentry was out of earshot.

"Probably doesn't want you finding your way back to the hospital for the next six weeks, Harry."

"Get stuffed."

The gradient seemed to lessen and the candles that

adorned the stairway suddenly began to increase in number, until the space before us opened up both left and right, into one long corridor.

"What are they for?" queried Earnshaw, pointing to an oil drum refilled with water.

"They're there to check for vibrations. If they start shaking unexplained, then you'll want to get out. Sharpish."

"Gotcha."

There was a recess in the side of the corridor, a smaller one than I had anticipated, but still sizeable enough for three bunkbeds.

A couple of candles flickered gently as they sensed the extra presence of three other bodies in the tunnel. The flickering disturbed the reading lights of two men, both sat on the top bunk of the two far beds, who simultaneously dropped what they were reading and inspected the shadows that had interrupted them.

They did not make for their weapons, nor turn around in a start, the men down here were far less jumpy than their contemporaries up on the surface.

The light of the candle steadied somewhat, so that it was no more than a slight sway, which was good enough to stop the letters of a book from dancing around the page. The older man of the two went back to reading his book, while the other continued to stare at his visitors without offering up any sort of a greeting.

"Are you the rats?" asked McKay, his abrupt Scotch tones sounding ten times as harsh and rude in the confines of the tunnel walls. Unsurprisingly, he succeeded in nothing other than turning the other man back to his letter writing.

Undeterred, McKay tried again, "Are you the clay-kickers?"

Again, he was ignored, which immediately got his back up.

"Oi, I said—"

"Are you from the 173rd Tunnelling Company, boys?"

It seemed all they wanted was a little recognition as humans. The younger of the two, turned his head towards us.

"That's right." His voice was ghostlike and faded, as if it had seen better days, and now each syllable he uttered was strenuous and drawn out.

"Who are you?" spoke the other bed-bound figure, without looking up from his book.

It was McKay's turn to ignore them, "Are you the moles that are going to be placing explosives under the German lines in a few nights' time?"

The younger mole continued to stare at us, like he was waiting for the older man's approval before speaking again. This was beginning to become painful, we were going to be here all night if they stubbornly refused to give up any information.

"I'm Sergeant Andrew Ellis. We heard about you lot in one of our briefings earlier."

"What do you want, a medal?" growled the older man, as he turned on his axis so that he was lying on his side, staring at us.

He was a much older man than I would have expected, in his early fifties at the most generous of estimates. His face was rough and uneven, like he had been at the business end of many collapsed mines. Maybe that was why he was coming across as so rude, the collapse had affected his brain.

The younger lad was not in much better condition. His hands were covered in blisters and scrapes, his face in similar nick to what must have been his father figure around here.

They seemed to have little to no regard for other human beings, so I didn't think I would be getting anywhere very fast by pulling rank and using the Sergeant card on them. I doubted that they would even struggle to stand to attention if Lord Kitchener himself was to descend the stairs to inspect them. We were going to get nowhere with these boys particularly fast.

"Is it true you lot are paid six times more than what we pack-horses get?"

A smirk appeared on the older clay-kicker's face, "From what I've been told. About five or six."

"Gits..." muttered Earnshaw, "Where can I get a transfer?"

The clay-kickers began to chuckle, as did Earnshaw, which slowly eased the tension.

"What do you reckon, Collins? This one would last, oh I don't know, a day?"

"If that," retorted Collins, the younger tunneller.

"You're joking, ain't ya? Look at me, I could do just as well as you with a bit of training!"

"Now that, I would like to see," I chipped in, which was met with disapproval from Earnshaw, but nothing but chuckles from the tunnellers.

I began to look around the corridor that we were stood in, drinking in the silence underneath the surface of the war, a silence that I had not experienced in a good many months. It was almost bliss down here.

The older man caught me having a good stare at his surroundings and began to grow inquisitive. Obviously, the draw of his book had finally been superseded.

"Why are you actually here?" he said, the smile disappearing from his face as quickly as it had appeared.

"We're the raiders. We were briefed earlier about a plan that involved both of us. We go over and raid the Germans and you are due to blow them up. Correct?"

"Correct. But why are you here?"

"We wanted to see the tunnels. Where you intend to put the explosives. We were curious."

"Nosey more like."

"That too."

He paused for a moment, as if waiting to pass judgement on a heinous crime.

"We can't show you. Too dangerous. Too crowded. We've got a lot of bodies working down there," he pointed towards one of the offshoots of which at least four could be seen from where I was stood. "This is as far as you lads will go, I'm afraid."

We must have looked disappointed.

"Come here, follow me."

He hopped from his bunk and guided us down the corridor, before ducking through a doorway to his right, which opened up into a small room. The room was sparsely populated, with a few unlevel tables and rickety old chairs. But down here, it was like having your own private room at the Ritz.

"The charges and mines are all set and ready to go. We just have to check on them regularly to make sure they are not damp. It took us nearly two days to get them all in place."

"It's going to make quite the explosion," chipped in Collins.

"Quite. We have other boys extending the other tunnels as we speak. Your explosion is merely a diversion. The Germans won't expect us to build the same tunnels twice. Not after we've blown them sky high. The brass are preparing for an offensive in this sector."

"We're just waiting for the order," piped in Collins, as if everything that he said was merely an echo of what the older man already divulged.

We smoked and chatted for the best part of an hour, to the point where we almost forgot where we were.

Both men, as well as many of their colleagues had been miners, from all around Britain. Some were from Sheffield and the coal mines, while others were from all parts of Wales that I could think of. Others still were sewerage workers, who had an incredible knowledge of how to build the structurally sound tunnels. It was all quite fascinating to laymen like us.

A low, aggressive rumble suddenly shook the foundations around us, and I watched in a panic as small avalanches of dirt suddenly fell from the ceiling and walls, dusting my feet in a light covering.

We waited for the candles to steady once more, before anyone spoke.

"Reckon it's time we made our move now, Andrew?"

"Yeah. Probably."

The tunnellers looked visibly disappointed.

"Before you go," Collins erupted, "how about a quick toast? To a job well done?"

"It's not done yet."

"To good luck then."

I didn't need too much persuasion, once I had got the sniff of a drink.

"To good fortune?" suggested Collins.

"And the end of the war," grumbled McKay.

"Oh, I'll definitely drink to that one!"

We drank up together, before beginning our farewells to one another.

"Get it right," pleaded McKay as we began to shake hands at the foot of the stairwell. "Make sure those mines go up. If you get it wrong, we'll all be dead in no time."

"You're not the only ones mate."

It was a fair point. This war was equally deadly for us all, it didn't matter if you were forty feet below the ground or crawling towards the enemy's frontline. They wanted us all dead.

9

It was a feeling that I was now all too familiar with, but I wished that I wasn't.

It wasn't so much the anticipation of going over that scared me now, but the non-existent guilt that I would feel when one of my team was left on the German side of the line. I felt the anguish of my own selfishness even more on that night, owing to the added responsibility that I now found upon my shoulders. Everyone, including Captain Arnold, would now be looking to me as an example; for guidance, for courage.

I stomped my feet in the slightly sticky mud, trying to push some blood into them and get my feeling back. It wasn't a particularly cold night, but my extremities were cold and clammy, as the worry in my gut built up and up, to the point where it was threatening to bubble over.

I checked that everything that might save my life was ready. My Webley was slipping all over the place in my sweaty palm, and I made certain for the fourteenth time that it was clear and that I was unlikely to get any stoppages.

I pricked my finger into one of the sawn-off nails that had been hammered into the club that was in my right hand, the points sharpened to such a degree that I could have drawn blood if I was to apply a little more pressure.

Finally, I checked that my rifle was still attached to its sling and that the sling itself was still attached to my body. I gave it a stern tug as I made sure that I was going to be able to crawl and roll without it coming loose.

I did the same with the cloth bandolier, that was strapped across my chest, and checked again that I had rounds in every single place that I could stuff them.

It felt oddly reassuring to be taking my rifle with me. It wasn't something that I had been accustomed to, but its presence, pressing into my back, was something that I managed to take great comfort from.

I had it so that I could use it for the second phase of our little excursion, if I made it that far. Of which I wasn't hopeful.

We were all under strict instructions not to stop to help a wounded man on any account, the only exception being to assist him in relieving his rounds from his bandolier and placing them under your own protection. If a man was down, we would need all of the rounds that we could muster.

As my feet splashed around in the sopping mud, I began to think of the boys that were forty odd feet below us. I wondered if they were as nervous as I was, the volatile charges all set without mishap and no injuries to speak of.

I hoped that they would be okay and that they would see the rest of this war out in one piece.

I began to tap my feet a little bit harder, and even contemplated stomping them in order to get some sort of a signal to them. I wanted them to know that I was thinking about them. I hoped that they were giving us lads some thoughts as well.

I imagined them going through their final preparations, readying themselves for the almighty explosion that was to come. I pictured young Collins being the one who was volunteered for the final checks of the piles of explosives and mines that were being used, his scared, timid little face flickering around as one lone candle lit his way.

I supposed that it wouldn't be too long now before they evacuated the tunnels completely, just in case any of the others happened to cave in as a result of the tremors. I recalled that they had dug other, auxiliary passages, ready to blow the Germans up for a second time, in line with an offensive, and I fired up a quick prayer that they all remained intact. Otherwise, all their hard work would have been for nothing.

Bob was glaring at me and I tried to ignore his unshaking stare for as long as I possibly could. Instinctively, I stopped tapping my feet around in the mud, as I knew that the slightest thing could set him off nowadays, and unless he had lost his memory, I was certain that me putting a bullet in his side wasn't too far from his mind right now. I hoped that he wasn't planning any kind of retaliation.

Make sure you keep him in front of you at all times. Just in case.

I did feel bad. I may not have shown it in actions, but I did feel some remorse towards him and what I had put him through. Shooting him had been an unintentional side effect of the pressures and strains that I had felt recently.

Part of me felt like I should really apologise to him, not necessarily for wounding him, but for the position that I had put him in, the one where he felt like he might have to go above my head if I did not change.

If I was to apologise for what I had done, I knew that he wouldn't have accepted it anyway. Bob was the kind of man who expected, demanded even, actions with words, and he would immediately have held his palm out waiting for the hip flask to land in it as soon as I apologised.

And I simply wasn't ready to give the flask up just yet. It wasn't just a dependence now, but a talisman. I still hadn't been killed while I had it.

GRHMN.

The engraved letters felt even more pronounced as I rubbed over its surface in my pocket. Its surface was warm on account of the fact that I continued to rub it for many more minutes after Bob's gaze had diverted from my face.

I was going to need it tonight. Everyone was. I just wished that they understood that all of their lives depended on it in one way or another.

I picked up Bob's baton of staring, as I took in the few facial features that he still had under all the grease and burnt cork. He was still quite a good-looking chap, despite the tiredness that seemed to make his face sag in the most depressing of fashions.

Despite the differences that had arisen in recent weeks, he was still a good man and I was grateful that he was a caring and compassionate NCO, as it was something that I couldn't manage to get my head around. Men died in war, so what was the point in becoming attached to them?

A small wisp of blonde hair was hastily tucked back under the woollen hat that was perched on his head, the same kind of hat that had begun to itch away at my scalp in the most uncomfortable degree.

"McKay, when we do get over there, what is it that you want me to do? Search for anything or keep watch?"

Hamilton's voice was clear and gentlemanly, a good old-fashioned English accent to boot. It was not as evolved and eloquent as Captain Arnold's, but he wasn't far off. Give it a couple more years and I was sure he would get there.

That was, of course, if he was to spend the next few years in the company of other gentlemen, and not, as was the case, with men like McKay.

"Look, Hamilton. Will you give it a rest? Your job will be to kill every single German you see tonight. It's not that difficult is it? Is your skull thicker than ours or something?"

Hamilton looked to the floor, sheepishly. He had liked asking questions, lots of them, particularly of McKay, for whatever reason.

He had even questioned the use of the weapons that we now brandished, having the same moral dilemma that I had when I had first joined the team.

He, like me, had chosen the bayonet and a revolver for his first raid, whereas I had progressed onto the far more medieval, but incredibly effective cosh, sharpened nails and all. It seemed barbaric, but it was no more barbaric than a Vickers gun spitting out over four hundred rounds in one minute.

"Leave him alone, McKay. Come on now," I said with a grin. "He's only trying to learn. We were all there once."

"I didn't ask so many stupid questions though."

They weren't stupid. They were completely logical, it was just Hamilton had the guts to voice them all.

He was keen to learn and had been acutely aware that the training he had received would more than likely be vastly inadequate, the minute he stepped off the trench ladder. He was a good lad, if a little naïve.

There was a strange attraction to the chap; the non-drinking, non-smoking, Anglican boy who had for some reason humbled himself to join the ranks in the army. He had excelled in the infantry and had still remained at the lowly rank of a private.

If his ability was anything like his hunger to learn, then this boy could have been a general in a matter of months. I was sure his ability would be more than put to the test in a matter of hours.

The Captain clicked his revolver shut and checked his watch.

"I reckon he's the sort of chap that would hand his own mother over to the police, if he suspected she had done something. What do you reckon?"

He nodded his head towards Hamilton.

"Yes. I can see him doing that sort of thing. A very headstrong type of lad."

"His back is incredibly straight. Everything has to be right. One of the reasons that I chose him."

I thought it was an incredibly odd criteria to have and immediately began arching my own back, pushing my shoulders back to try and emulate the humble aristocrat.

Captain Arnold pulled back on the sleeve of his tunic to take a long hard look at his watch.

"Ready, Sergeant?"

It took a few seconds to realise that he was talking to me.

I was now the Captain's right-hand man, it would be me that he ran everything past now. He was expecting me to step up, to fill Hughes' boots and to be on hand with ideas and plans. It suddenly made me feel incredibly inadequate.

The vague, almost half-hearted pangs of guilt and sadness that I had experienced at Hughes' death suddenly re-emerged, this time far stronger and more convicting than ever before.

I wanted him back.

"Yes, Sir. Absolutely."

He looked at me, with a slight smile on his face.

"You got that hip flask with you, Sergeant Ellis?"

"Of course, Sir."

He chuckled softly, before facing front, muttering under his breath.

"Good...Good..."

I wondered if Bob had been to him with his grievances and whether or not he knew about the quivering hand and excruciating headaches. If he did, he didn't seem to care. Maybe the hip flask had become as comforting to him as it had to me. It was possible it had become our lucky charm, that's why he would have refused to say anything about it.

Deep down, Captain Arnold was as superstitious as the rest of us.

It wasn't the only piece of additional kit that I had on my person. I had re-stuffed the German flag down the front of my tunic. I was convinced that it might bring me some good fortune and, even if it didn't, it wasn't an eventuality that I wanted to put to the test on this operation.

If all else failed, it would at least give me a little extra protection against a German bayonet.

I didn't know what had possessed me to bring the flag with me, but I supposed that a part of me was hoping to make amends with Bob, if he found out that I had returned it. It was a pathetic attempt at trying to go back to how I used to be, but it had made me feel ever so slightly better as I stuffed it into my tunic.

"Chaps," rasped the Captain, as loud as he dared, "let's get this done. Execute the plan to the letter please. As few casualties as possible."

I wondered suddenly if he had been in the same briefing as us, and as I looked around at the perplexed faces, I realised that the others thought he had been joking too.

At least one of us would die tonight, if not all of us. The plan was a ridiculous one.

Nevertheless, we were soldiers, good ones and so we unquestioningly followed our orders.

As I stepped out into No Man's Land, I strained my eyes as I always did, trying to spot the accompanying men emerging from the slits in the ground at the same time.

I never saw them, but I could almost feel their presence, walking alongside me towards the enemy.

Tonight, they would be pivotal. They needed to cause as much chaos and confusion as they possibly could.

The more confusion, the larger the chance that men like me, and the rest of our squad would stay alive. At least for a few more minutes.

10

I didn't have a home anymore. I couldn't remember my life before I joined the army, even though it had been less than a year ago.

My parents no longer encompassed my thoughts like they had done previously. Everything that I now did was for myself, purely and selfishly. It wasn't because I didn't care for my mother or father, or in fact any of the troops that I encountered, but because that was just how it was in this war.

You looked out for the other men around you, but the reason you were still living was because you had put yourself first and not them. It was a fact that I wasn't entirely proud of, but it was a fact, nonetheless.

I was more of a wanderer now, not really having any kind of a resting place or somewhere to call home. But I had somewhere to rest my head each night and wake up come morning.

The closest that I had to something that felt like home was standing in an enemy trench, with bodies lying all about me. It sounded brutal and almost detestable, even to myself, but I had become hooked, I lived to journey across No Man's Land and into the enemy frontline.

So, to all intents and purposes, it could be said that I felt like I was back at home. I had made myself comfortable here and I would continue to do so.

It felt strange to say it, but I had missed the excitement of going out on a raid. It had only been a week since the last one that we had journeyed out on, but I had been pining to go over the bags once again and get stuck right in.

The air was exceptionally cold for the time of year and I knew that if I was to roll on my back, a perfect complement of stars would be twinkling away above me, gratefully taking in my gaze and appreciation.

But there was no opportunity to do that. There hadn't been any time to appreciate any of the finer things in life the minute I stepped off the troop ship into France. In fact, it felt that it was impossible to have a world away from the frontline, where acres upon acres of farmland rolled on for hours completely uninterrupted.

It was utterly inconceivable that there were trees, somewhere in the world, that hadn't been burned to the ground or shredded into thousands of pieces by incessant artillery. It was almost impossible to believe that once upon a time, it was even probable that you might have seen a little blackbird in the tree in the morning, seeking out a worm or two for its young.

The whole idea of a world away from the decimated canvas of the frontline was impossible.

The unfortunate truth was that I had got used to the

barrenness of the landscape. I had become accustomed to seeing trees, blackened and cracked, and fields nothing more than a large bucket of mud.

It did not seem to affect me anymore, my love of nature completely vanquished at the first sound of falling artillery.

I had got used too to the death that accompanied the destruction. Men had fallen all around me, their agonising screams bellowing in my ears, but none of them were carried with me for any longer than it took to digest a bit of bully beef.

I thought nothing of death.

All of this had made me a better soldier, but a worse man.

I reflected on all this as I stared at the two corpses that had, until about three seconds before, been alive and kicking. Very alive and very kicking.

One of them had been a short, stumpy little fellow, like he had accidentally fallen into the army and had been leant some of his big brother's clothes. I began to chuckle, before I rebuked myself.

This isn't a joke. He is young enough to be someone's little brother.

In some ways, I was glad that I had dispatched of him the way that I had done, a swift knife blade to the throat. Several times over. It had been relatively quick for him. I hoped that it had been painless, but I knew that it wouldn't have been.

The other man that lay at my feet hadn't been so lucky.

I had given him a whacking great crack over the side

of his face with the wooden cosh that I held tightly in my right hand.

He'd had his helmet on, and as such, I had to attack him at such an angle that I would have been effective.

The wooden truncheon on its own wouldn't have been enough, which was why I was mightily glad that I had invested in some sizeable nails to bash into it for just such an occasion.

The first blow had embedded the rusting nails into his cheekbone, and I ripped out large chunks of flesh as I had withdrawn from his skin. The second caught the back of his hand as he reached up to touch his face, which almost seem to pin it to his skin.

The remaining blows had been a mixture of stabs and whacks, as I alternated between movements to try and put this man to sleep as quickly as possible. I liked to think I was doing it in some sort of a humane gesture. But it wasn't.

I manoeuvred myself away from the bodies, at least to stop dwelling on how they died but, at most, out of a sense of duty to keep everyone safe.

In the last few raids, all of the offending parties had been caught out by a hiding German in one of their dugouts. It had accounted for many deaths and even more close calls in recent weeks.

We couldn't afford a death tonight, not at this stage anyway. It was a long night ahead, and we needed to be at full strength for as much of it as possible.

I stood guard over the doorway, revolver at hip height and pointing into the darkened room, my spiky truncheon resting offensively on my shoulder, ready to be brought down hard on someone's skull.

No one is making it out of here alive tonight.

As I stood there, I resisted the urge to brush the dirt and mud from the underside of my nose, that was tickling away and threatening to make me sneeze. Instead, I lifted my head slightly, allowing the next wave of muddy hail to disturb the dirt and restore some element of comfort.

The noise inside the trench was deafening, with the howling hellhounds that were pummelling the second line of trenches slightly further back, but also doing a sterling job of making sure the Germans kept their heads down.

Part of me wanted them desperately to stop, as I was beginning to feel myself go mad but, at the same time, I wanted them so badly I was prepared to put up with the racket for a little while longer. I didn't feel like advancing into the night without them just yet.

"Hamilton, here," I rasped over the noise, just as the new raider swept past me. He was always asking questions about what he should do, so I gave him something to do. "Look over this dugout. Make sure no one comes out. Got it?"

"Yes, Sergeant."

I shuffled my way up the trench, treading on the outsides of my feet to try and preserve them for the utter torture that I would be putting them through later on.

A little bit of pain now could be the difference between living and dying. Or that's what I told myself anyway.

I ran my eyes over everyone that was in the trench. Everyone seemed fine.

Bob scooted past me.

"You okay, Bob?"

"Golden," came his curt reply.

We had fallen out, but it didn't mean I wanted him to come to any harm. He was still one of my best friends after all. Just one of my friends that I was going to try and get transferred at the earliest opportunity.

"Sir," I called out, as I reached the imposing shadow of Captain Arnold, "we have about ninety seconds left. Ninety seconds, Sir," I repeated.

I knew there was little to no chance of him listening to what I had said and, even if he did, I doubted that it had registered in his mind. He was that focused on what he was doing.

He had found a leather briefcase belonging to an officer somewhere, and he was slowly making his way through it, reading everything from high command orders to personal love letters. I knew that he was trying to commit as much of it to memory as was possible, including the passages of affection from Munich.

He built up a nice pile of stuff on top of the case, before he began lighting them all with a match and within seconds, they were crackling away nicely. I did the same with a similar pile that I had quickly created.

We had to make this look like a genuine raid, at least for the next hour or so. The Germans had to believe as far as possible that we had retreated back out into No Man's Land, taking as much intelligence as was possible.

But, at the same time, we were trying to cause chaos and confusion, with a side order of complete demoralisation. By burning the letters and orders, we would hopefully achieve all three goals. Plus, we didn't want the

Germans to take their own intelligence back from our cold, stiff bodies. It was better this way.

"Sir, thirty seconds. We need to make a move."

"Okay, Sergeant Ellis. Let's go."

I tapped McKay on the shoulder and motioned that we were about to start our next phase. The phase that would get us killed.

"Hamilton," I croaked, right into his ear, so that he would have heard me even if he was profoundly deaf, "we're moving. Come on."

"Yes, Sergeant."

He was an obedient type of man, the kind that would have made an excellent servant, had he not been the one to command them himself back at home. Every utterance that came out of my mouth seemed to be met with an obliging "Yes, Sergeant," in his silky, soft tones.

He made me feel more important. Too important in fact to die. I was beginning to like him.

So far, we were in the midst of a roaring success. No one was dead. No one was injured. And we hadn't fired a single shot yet. We had our maximum number of men and rounds. Good. We were definitely going to need them.

"Everyone knows the plan," I shouted as we huddled our heads together for a moment, our breaths all intertwining into one hot, smelly concoction. "Hard and fast through their lines, don't stop for any man that goes down. Do not miss your targets. You *have* to hit them. More now than ever before. Got it?"

As I finished, the howling dwindled rapidly to nothing but a silence. The silence was filled by my own mind, so used to hearing the screams that it was all I heard for the next ten seconds afterwards. We all stood stock still as we allowed our eardrums to catch up with reality.

I could almost imagine the gunners quickly restocking their weapons, disposing of the used shells and replenishing their piles with brand new ones. Their job wasn't over for the night yet, they had almost as much to do as we did. They needed to be more alert than us.

The silence seemed to increase to the point where I began to long for the artillery back. I preferred noise, I always had done, it just meant that there was something to cover you if you accidentally made a noise, like a cough or sneeze. When it was silent, a simple thing like an awkward footstep could be the difference between going undetected and having an entire army bundle on top of you.

It was so quiet, that I was certain I could hear the Brits back in our frontline going about their night-time routines, listening out for the firefight that would soon flare up on the frontline that we were creating.

I eradicated everything. I needed to be able to run, hard and fast, while picking targets at the same time. It was risky. But it had to be done.

This was war.

This was what I loved.

11

"Is everyone ready?"

No.

My immediate response to the Captain's question was not one that would be deemed unusual, and if I was to look Captain Arnold in the eye, then I was fairly certain his answer would be exactly the same.

What we were preparing to do went against everything in innate human nature, against everything that I had ever been taught how to do. Instead of running away from danger, I was about to go in search of even more of it.

I had been raiding for many months now and had consequently become accustomed to the fear of scraping my stomach over No Man's Land, ignoring the bodies and decaying remnants of human flesh that lay about out there. But the idea of going further into the German lines was a notion that I was so petrified of, that I didn't know how to control myself.

A blinding headache had stretched across my head,

reaching from ear to ear, and the quiver in my hand had returned the minute I realised that I was not actually dreaming. This was actually about to happen.

The distant rumbles of far away artillery carried on somewhere in the distance and I found myself longing to be underneath those shells. If I was there, I would be able to find some sort of cover, I would be able to get under the ground and wait until the storm had settled.

But, being here, I had no choice but to carry on further, especially as I was convinced that the Captain would shoot anyone who refused to go with him.

I locked eyes with Bob for a moment and, for a second, we shared a time that was reminiscent of days gone by. The days when I had relied on him for courage, instead of the hip flask. In a time when I was nervous about every far-off rumble, or distant sniper's crack.

I needed him now. He had always been my friend, he had always been fighting alongside me. The only reason why he had pulled me up on the things that he had done was for my own good. It was to keep me alive. Maybe I had misjudged him.

There was something inside my gut though, that continued to tell me that he needed to be transferred away from the rest of us. Maybe it wasn't for the good of the team like I had reasoned before. Maybe it was for his own good. I wanted him to live.

And this job continually kept asking us to die.

"Ready?" repeated the Captain impatiently, as he locked eyes with me as if I had let him down in some way. He expected a sense of fear in all of them, of cowardice maybe, but from me, he wanted nothing but bravery and determination. It was something that I was unsure I would be able to give him.

It had been the late Sergeant, the one who used to wear the very same stripes that I now wore on my jacket, that had told me something that sprang into my head as we stood there.

The Captain does not like half-hearted volunteers.

And now wasn't the time to get on his bad side. He couldn't send us away to our billet here or stick us on some mundane and frankly unnecessary mission.

Out here, we had to be friends. Because, if we weren't his friends, we were his enemies. And we all knew what he did to his enemies.

"Yes, Sir. We're ready."

He gave us all a look in turn as if to say, "You're sure about that?" before he thought better of it and simply nodded.

That was it. That was the sign. We were committed now. There was simply no going back.

It was entirely possible that I had just signed the bottom of my very own death warrant.

I looked around the faces that peered out from the darkness around me. All of them looked as though they were raring to go, if not completely petrified at the same time.

Even the new boy, Hamilton, looked as though he was ready to finally get stuck into this war and begin delivering some of that propaganda-fuelled fury that he had pent up in him somewhere.

I wondered for a second if he had any kind of an idea of what would lurk for him on the other side of this trench wall, the vastness of death and destruction on a scale of which that rivalled Pompeii. I debated whether he had known that he would have to get up close and extremely personal with this enemy, before ripping his throat out or simply bludgeoning him to death.

It was far easier to do it from afar, through the sights of a Lee-Enfield, than to do it with a bayonet. At least that way you never really saw the fear in their eyes.

I must have been showing a fair amount of fear in my own face, I was convinced that it was what was causing the burning agony in my eyes and across my forehead. But I put it all down to the fact that we were about to venture further into, and behind enemy lines, than any other soldier had done previously before in this war. Even the Germans had not been gutsy enough to do this yet.

Every time I put my head down on my bed in the upstairs room of the *Café de Fleurs,* I had felt incredibly safe, to the point where I was able to forget about the war. After tonight, I would go to sleep in constant fear that we would now be in range of a retaliatory enemy raid along similar sorts of lines.

We were being asked to travel seven miles out of the trench system. There was no hope of reinforcements or artillery to back us up when we got there.

It was madness.

Slowly, we moved off, with a sizeable gap between the first man and the next. It would be beneficial for us all if we gave ourselves that extra half second to react to the figure who had suddenly appeared from a dugout, or the sentry that would block our route until he was dealt with.

It also helped us to stay in the strictest possible silence, as there was no way that we could talk or whisper to one another being so far apart. It made me feel uncomfortably aware of all the immediate sounds around me, each thumping footstep, louder than the distant artillery, was solely my doing. It was no one else's responsibility.

As we moved through the communication lines that ran perpendicular to the frontline trench, I made a note to try and stay as anonymous as possible.

We had all been stripped of our insignia, we were simply in dark coloured clothes now, that may or may not have been a British uniform.

Each of us kept our heads as low as we dared, without compromising our ability to anticipate what was about to head our way.

To the very best of our ability, we were trying to be shadows. But I knew that eventually, the cloak that we were trying to pull over ourselves would eventually be thrown from us, and we would be called to fight, just like all the other times that we had hit the German frontline.

There was still an element of hope in the pit of my stomach, a sense of optimism that had still withstood the storm and refused to be dwindled, despite everything that I had been through.

There was still a hope that I might actually make it through the next half an hour, and then after that, the next hour or so. If I did that, then I might actually make it back over No Man's Land, I might actually make it back to see Porky Paul in the *Café de Fleurs*.

The hope began to take root in my gut and began to provide me with an inch of confidence that was so desperately needed.

It slowly morphed into what could only be described as a wishful optimism, as I imagined the Germans in the reserve lines as old, fatigued men; each one of them cleaning his rifle at the moment we struck, so they were unable to fire upon us before we disappeared.

It was at that moment that I remembered the advice that I had heeded for so long, the advice I had received from my first Sergeant.

Being hopeful got you nowhere in this war. In fact, the only place that it really got you was in a shallow grave shared with fifteen other men. It was that complacency that was creeping up on me that was going to get me killed.

You are going to die tonight. Remember that. Try and keep the rest of them alive at least.

I became more conscious of my surroundings for the first time, as I continued to bring up the rear of our snaking column as we delved deeper into the German lines.

I was following directly behind Hamilton, making sure that no one would sneak up on him and raise the alarm of our presence. My job was two-fold however, as I was constantly having to turn on my heel, to double check that we were not being followed, or about to walk into some sort of a trap.

I was losing ground with them though, and I became conscious that if I was to stay at this pace, then the others would simply advance without me. They had been told to stop for no one after all.

But I couldn't speed up for fear of making a mistake, as I undoubtedly would.

At that moment, as I turned on my heel to check what lurked behind us, I caught sight of a much darker shadow suddenly stepping into my own.

It was an enemy soldier. It just had to be. I would have to catch up with the others later on.

I was hoping to take him by surprise, but that was gone. He had already spotted me. He knew I was an enemy. I had the wrong kind of face.

He had the quicker reactions, his body suddenly enlarging as he lunged at me, the butt of his rifle connecting with my chest with an almighty force. That was his first mistake, or maybe it had been the darkness which meant that he hadn't struck me across the face.

I staggered for a moment, breathless, before I swung my revolver-wielding hand towards his cheekbone. I connected well, with a dull crack and I thought I had sent him to the floor.

But all that met me was the well-timed, well-aimed thump of his rifle, this time connecting with my jaw perfectly. Blood gushed to my mouth so fast that I thought I was about to drown.

I flew onto my back, losing grip of both my revolver and my wooden truncheon. He landed on top of me, a knife in his hand ready to finish me off.

This is it. This is how you're going to die.

I wasn't ready to die just yet. I couldn't stand the thought of the others not knowing what had happened to me, until they came across my corpse in years to come, when this trench inevitably became a part of No Man's Land.

I reached out, and gripped the wooden handle of an entrenching tool, which soon found itself bashing the poor man over the skull, repeatedly, until his body fell from mine.

Breathless, my chest feeling like it was going to crack

open at any second, I rolled on top of him. For a moment, I thought I was about to vomit all over him but conjured up enough energy from somewhere, deep within the pits of my existence, to stay focused.

I had no weapon to speak of. The entrenching tool was good, but it wasn't going to be able to kill him from this position.

Blood leaked from his head and I imagined that he had a headache similar, if not worse, than my own.

As I searched through my options, I knew I had to do something, and the pressure that I was putting on his throat with my forearm simply wasn't going to be enough to put this to bed.

So, with my left arm still squeezing onto the man's neck, I pushed the thumb of my right hand into his eyeball, firmly.

He began to howl apishly, which was subdued significantly by the lack of air in his lungs. Blood gushed from the side of his eyeball, as he scratched away at my wrist and arms, trying all sorts of methods to simply get me off.

It allowed me some time to take a quick look around for my weapons, or anything else that I could make use of.

My revolver and truncheon had fallen some way away, too far for me to grab and get back to the man within a reasonable window.

Then, my eyes fell on what would become my primary weapon. The German's bayonet, not four feet away from where we lay grappling.

I flung my legs over his chest, as I lunged for the bayonet, taking the pressure off his eyeball for the first time.

He screamed in an uproarious agony, so loud that I

wouldn't have been surprised if the Kaiser himself had heard it in Berlin.

It was cut short though, as the bayonet was thrust into the man's neck, several times, before one, final piercing blow through his heart, which put up far more of a resistance than I could have ever imagined.

I had done what I had needed to. I had to move on now. Forget about what I had done, what I had become. I needed to focus once more. I needed to remember that I was going to die tonight. It just hadn't been my time, that was all.

Now, I was all alone, with no idea how far ahead the others were. They probably hadn't even noticed that I was gone.

There was another pressing concern. Every minute longer that we spent in this trench meant that we were a minute closer to being sent sky high, with the rest of the trenches.

And we had no clue who held the keys over when exactly the mines would be blown up.

I needed to knuckle down. I needed to get out of here.

12

My whole body was tense as I continued to make my way through the trench alone. My revolver pointing dead ahead at hip height, my truncheon held high above my head ready for what might lay around the corner, I advanced quickly and aggressively as I tried to catch up with the others.

The artillery that was now screaming over my head continued to howl, as I tried to focus every inch of my being dead ahead of me, I had no time nor energy to turn around and check what was coming up behind me. Even if someone was coming up, I felt like I was moving too fast for them to catch me now. I was like a bolt of lightning in the dark.

The only time my gaze deviated from dead ahead of me was when I glanced down at the bodies that now littered the trenches. They filled me with an almost subhuman emotion of pride and comfort.

The artillery barrage was now creeping forward,

slowly smashing into anything and everything that it could find. But I noticed something about the bodies.

These bodies didn't look as though they had been smashed to pieces by the artillery, nor did they look like they had been buried alive by the avalanche of mud and dirt that came with every explosion.

Each one of the corpses seemed to have been impaled on a long, sharp piece of steel. It was a sign I was on the right track, I was heading in the right direction. I wasn't lost.

My colleagues had been here, and they had done their job brilliantly in my absence. I continued to advance confidently, knowing full well that they would have cleared as many bodies as they could out of my path.

Before too long however, the Germans would begin to emerge from their bunkers as the artillery moved on further behind them. They would begin to see the body count we had left behind, and the friends, that they had once known as bubbly and excitable individuals, were now lying at the bottom of the trench, with blood gushing from their chest.

They were going to know that they had visitors in their lines. But more than that, they were going to know that the visitors that had been in the frontline trenches not half an hour before, were now advancing deeper and deeper into their reserve lines, trying to cause as much havoc and chaos as they possibly could.

We were leaving behind a trail of breadcrumbs so large that an outsider might have mistaken them for chunks of human flesh. They were going to know we were there.

They were going to know I was there.

My knees ached as I continued to power my way through the trenches, turning at right angles every twenty seconds or so. The headache, that had been simmering away at the back of my head for hours, intensified dramatically, and I was now fighting off the physical pain as well as the mental pain I was putting myself through.

I couldn't find my comrades, I knew that they had been there, but I was certain that I should have caught up by now. There was no way that I had been engaged in fighting with the German for that long.

With a wave of nausea about the potential loss of my accomplices, I rounded a corner, revolver up at my chest height.

I was confronted by shadowy figure.

"Hamilton."

"Sergeant."

I lowered my quivering revolver, inching my finger away from the trigger, relieved that I hadn't just put a bullet into the uptight face of the junior aristocracy.

"Are you okay, Sergeant?" Rasped Hamilton rather too loudly for my liking. He seemed like a caring enough sort, but that had probably had something to do with the fact that he saw me as the figure that would keep him alive. In the same way that I'd seen Sergeant Needs and Sergeant Hughes when I had first started.

I waved his comment away and began to move quicker to catch up with the rest of the team.

As we advanced, in our reunited snake-like pattern, I began to notice that the trenches were becoming shallower. In the frontline I had been able to stand tall, and knew that there were sandbags and an elevated bank of mud that would keep my head below the parapet.

But here, my head and shoulders poked out proudly if I was to stand up straight. As such, we all ran hunched over, our heads up, to double check that we weren't about to run into a wave of German reinforcements.

The closer we got to the end of the trenches, the closer we got to the very extreme of our artillery.

That meant that the Germans' heads wouldn't be able to be kept down for much longer. In a matter of minutes, we were going to be totally on our own. And part of me was looking forward to that.

Bob, who was leading the advance, suddenly dropped to one knee and waited for the rest of us to catch up. Once we had huddled together, I began to make out his voice, carried softly through the darkness, a total contradiction to what his voice sounded like over the last few weeks. The gruff and often rude tones that I had become so used to, were gone. He was speaking softly now, like a vicar trying to comfort the grieving relative.

"What is it, Sargent?" Queried Captain Arnold.

"I think it would be pertinent if we were to use our rifles now, Captain."

"Agreed."

One at a time we worked our way down the line, as we swung our Lee-Enfield rifles off our shoulders and checked that they were ready to go. The brass rounds were already in, they had to be so that they could dig us all out of a hole if we had needed them to.

The wild but worried look reappeared in the Captain's eyes. He was subdued for a moment, as he began to lose himself in the side alleys of his own mind. I was becoming worried about him, with every minute that passed he seemed to become more exhausted and more fearful of what lay around the corner. It was not like him at all, he was normally such a confident and sure man, but tonight he was convinced he was going to die, I could see that just from his eyes.

"Stay low. Stay quiet. Stay alert. You know what to do. Carried out the very best of your ability please, gentlemen. And, if it all goes to pot, it is every man for himself."

"If?" Hamilton chimed in, precariously.

"When," winked Earnshaw, mischievously. It did nothing to settle any of our nerves, especially Hamilton's. I had always liked the prospect of being able to work on my own, especially as I had a knack of winding everyone else up, so it seemed. But to hear Captain Arnold declare that it would be every man for himself, unnerved me to such a degree that I thought momentarily about running away, back to our lines.

That was all that needed to be said, each of us knew our duty, each one of us knew our responsibility, each one of us knew that we would die.

But we were prepared for it, it was what we had been put on this world to do.

"When you are ready then, Bob. Move off in your own time."

I knew that the same thought was going through all of our heads right now, we did not want to move off. We felt safe here. We felt like we might live if we stayed here.

But, as the final few fleeting shells of artillery began to drop around us, we knew that the Germans would soon be emerging from their warrens, like pesky moles once a farmer has gone to bed.

Obligingly, each one of us rose from our position and began to follow Bob, a similar sort of distance apart to the one that we had adopted earlier on. We continued to follow the wooden pathway that had been laid out for us by the Germans, the rickety old wooden boards doing everything they possibly could to slow us down.

As we passed a pair of low sandbagged walls, one either side of the path, I realised that we were back at ground level once more. The terrain here was completely flat, so flat in fact it reminded me of a snooker table that I'd seen used so often in the working men's club in my town. It was the first time that I thought of home in what must have been about three months.

I suddenly realised how all-encompassing this war had become. It was all that I could remember, it was all that I was focused on, it was the only thing that I was good at.

Our artillery had done a cracking job here, everything that had been above the ground was now flattened to lie just about three inches above it. It was the result of many months of hard work and also a few million shells.

It struck me as odd at how similar our frontlines and reserve lines were to the Germans'. Both armies were dug into the ground across the whole of the Western front, at a depth of seven or maybe eight feet. If you were then to move about a mile or so to the rear of each front line, the landscape was completely mimicked. Trees grew no taller than a stump, houses were nothing more than rubble and any existence of a previous way of life here had been completely eradicated.

We moved swiftly over the wooden pathway that sat undulating in the boggy fields all around us. We knew this was going to be a long track, with an estimated three mile walk to the artillery pieces, and then hopefully only another mile or so after that to our target.

I lost my footing several times as I stumbled and fell from the duckboards, that were trying to throw me off like some sort of stubborn mule. I found it progressively difficult to keep my head up the whole time, but I wanted to see what was coming next.

Captain Arnold was dead ahead of me and I watched as the butt of his rifle swung to and fro as he heaved himself forward. Suddenly, he stopped dead in his tracks throwing himself to the side of the board with a splash.

It was not something that we could think through or argue with him about. We all knew that we had to do the same.

I jumped.

I found myself lying face down in the mud, my rifle painfully tucked under my stomach as it felt like it was trying to advance into my rib cage.

We lay there as one body for what felt like hours, to the point where I began to raise my head to see what all the fuss was about. I became concerned that maybe it had been a mistake, and I had been seeing things, which had now led me to lying in a field somewhere behind German lines, completely on my own.

It did not take me long however to hear them, softly at first, but advancing rapidly on our position. Every gut feeling that I had told me that I had to roll away now, to avoid being seen, but I knew it would do more harm than good.

I had no way of protecting myself further now, this

was as much cover as I was going to be able to achieve. I knew the others would be feeling exactly the same.

I began hoping with every ounce of my energy that the darkness and the stillness of the night would afford me more cover than I thought that it might.

The sound of thumping footsteps coming ever closer to our position resounded out solemnly on the wooden boards, like a hangman's drum call. I felt like a man condemned, his head on the block waiting for the guillotine to sink downwards and into the back of my neck. I felt just as blind as that man.

Breathless words began to waft to my ears, and I wished that I was lying directly next to McKay, so that he was able to translate what was being said. It might have meant the difference between going on a ten-mile hike in the wrong direction, and a resounding success.

I lay as still as I possibly could, holding my breath for as long as my lungs seemed able. Just one exhalation of breath and the whispering cloud that came with it, could give away our position.

The freezing mud began to bite away at the front of my body, until it was completely numb of all the pain. It felt good for a while, to be in some sort of comfort, but quite quickly the numbness gave way to an agonising pain as my body tried to keep itself warm. I tried to switch off the trembling shivers that were threatening to get me killed.

I began to move my arm stretching down to withdraw my revolver, in the hope that I would have a few seconds to react before we were killed. In all likelihood though, we would be dead before we had even found out that we had been spotted.

The footsteps began to echo around in my head as they drew closer and closer. Just as I thought they would stop right above my head, I realised that they were actually thundering away in the opposite direction. We were safe. For now.

As the bodies continued to hammer away in the darkness towards their trenches, the warm smell of some sort of soup wafted to my nostrils as it was left hanging in the air.

All of a sudden, I became incredibly hungry, and the agonising aches of what felt like starvation began to take hold of my mind.

The Captain was the first up on his feet, kneeling for a moment with his rifle across his knee. He scanned the area warily for a moment, before turning to his invisible men that lay somewhere behind him.

"It's clear. Get up, let's go."

We did as we were told, only to throw ourselves into the freezing mud, just an arm's length away from advancing German soldiers, on three more separate occasions. It was only a matter of time before we were caught out.

The Captain suddenly skidded to a halt, as I thought we would have to repeat our routine of splashing into the mud and lying helpless as we waited to be found out. But this time he just stood and waited for us all to catch up.

"Over there," he whispered, arm outstretched in front of him and just off to his right side.

We all followed his gaze obediently, hoping that we might see the German high command headquarters, so that we could put an end to this war once and for all.

What we saw was totally different, yet not at all unexpected. We had studied the maps for hours upon hours, we felt like we knew their trench system like the back of our hand. But still, it felt odd to see it in the flesh.

Up ahead we could just about make out the licking flames of a fire. Instantaneously, I felt immensely jealous of the men who were gathered around it, I could almost see the warmth that they were enjoying, the warmth my body was crying out for.

That's not why you're here. Focus.

I began trying to switch on and take in the relevant information that was before me.

There were two fires from what I could see, around which stood at least four men apiece, arms outstretched over the burning furnace, smoke pouring into their eyes.

The silhouettes of the men around the fires flickered with intensity, as the flames danced around in the freezing midnight air. But it was the vague outlines that I could see behind them that I was particularly interested in, what we were all interested in.

As if an artist had faintly outlined his masterpiece, so the artillery guns appeared behind the heads of the flaming silhouettes.

We were close. We didn't have much further to go now. Maybe I would make it out of this one alive.

13

We were close now, so close that with a swift ejection of rounds the whole artillery piece would be silenced for a number of hours.

But I knew that wasn't our job that night, we had far bigger things to be worried about. It didn't relinquish any of my guilt however when the guns started opening up and I knew exactly where the four-inch shells were going to land.

I began wishing in earnest that there was some sort of early warning system that we could implement, in order to save countless British lives. I didn't want to have to journey back to our lines, only to witness the carnage and destruction of the British line, as men were carted around limbless, uniforms seared away from their skin.

Come on. That's not why you're here.

If we were to be successful, then there was a possibility that the artillery pieces in this area would be silenced for weeks, if not months. The lives of six men was such a small price to pay for such a large achievement.

I readjusted my thoughts and tried to take in as much of my surroundings as was possible, giving myself the best chance of survival but also success.

I tried to look beyond the darkness of the artillery guns and could make out a vague outline of something that I was unfamiliar with.

The Captain edged his way over to me, to consult with his new confidant about what our next move should be. It was a position that I was not yet comfortable with, and one that I felt I was wholly unqualified for, but Captain Arnold had expectations of me, and I knew that I must fulfil them.

"That's a locomotive," he muttered and for a moment I wondered if he was actually talking to me at all, or whether the meanderings of his mind had accidentally slipped out as his voice. "That must be a light railway behind those guns. That railway is what is supplying the shells falling in our sector of the line."

I wasn't entirely sure what I was meant to say in reply, besides my mind was totally elsewhere; I could not distract myself from the odd smell of what must have been the locomotive.

It was an odd smell of suffocating smoke but also of slightly sweetened grease, which made me feel nauseous yet exceedingly hungry at the same time. It was a strange phenomenon to me, and as such one that I could not shake my mind from.

"What do you think, Sergeant?"

I needed to quickly scan my knowledge of the area and try to pinpoint where exactly on the map we were, to ensure that the Captain was right. He wanted something constructive, not just the obliging affirmative that he would expect of any other soldier.

"We've done well to cover ground in such a time, Sir. Judging by our intelligence, we should only be a mile or two away from the supply dump now."

"Excellent."

The tired and worried look, that had been etched across his face in recent days, was in complete and utter contrast to the burning excitement that flared up in his eyes at the realisation. It must have been nice, I thought, to be able to enjoy what we were doing and not be so hung up on surviving to the next day that you could be so reckless, yet so brilliant a soldier.

He piped up again, "Not far to go then. All we need to do now then is vaguely follow that light railway track. That should take us right up to the supply dump."

His voice was still in a harsh whisper, but one that threatened to break out into an excited scream with the very next syllable that he uttered.

He could spot the weakness in his excitable state too, as he closed down his statement with a simple, "The target."

"All quite simple, really."

It was a risky moment, one that was fraught with feelings of having misjudged the Captain and visions of his anger at what I had said. Instead, I was met with a semi-approving stare, but was tinged with just the slightest hint of a smile.

But it was a look that told me never to use his catchphrase ever again. None of us had very much left thanks to this war and that catchphrase was the one thing that was his.

We both continued to survey the scene for a few moments more, in case we had missed anything that we had not seen on our first observations of the place. It was a time that was welcome for both the Captain and me, as we could spend a few moments in the quietness of our own minds, evaluating what we were about to do and what the Germans might do back at us.

The ensuing silence was one of two troubled men, who had a shared goal but also shared concerns.

"Do you think the men are up to it?"

He surprised me, not because of what he had asked, but because it was exactly the same question that I was asking myself.

None of the men were exactly fully fit for service. Bob and Earnshaw had only recently been wounded, and although they assured us that they were fighting fit, there was a degree of doubt that had crept into my mind in the few hours leading up to our raid. Once we had completed what we had set out to do, our job would turn from one of being quiet and discreet, to one of extreme violence and speed, and I wasn't entirely sure that they were capable of carrying it off.

Hamilton, through no fault of his own, was inexperienced and had no idea how quickly this sort of thing could go wrong. It was still so easy for me to recall the feelings of jubilation and satisfaction that I had entertained on my first raid, before the unexpected taught me about the humility that was required of a trench raider.

Even McKay, who was perhaps the most experienced and efficient among us, caused me a great deal of concern. It was not because of what had happened before, and the slight wobble that he had endured out in No Man's Land, but it was the fact that he felt like he needed to make amends for it, to redeem himself that made me wonder whether or not he would be able to keep a level head.

"Yes," I lied, "definitely. I couldn't think of anyone better qualified than these men."

He locked himself in his thoughts once more, before seemingly taking even himself by surprise.

"Have you got that hip flask, Ellis?"

"Yes, Sir."

"Get it out, will you?"

I did as I was told.

GRHMN.

It felt good to be able to get something out that meant so much to me, being so close to going into action. It was something that I had not risked before, but I knew that its contents would give me the courage that I needed to perform even better than I already had done.

I held it out for a moment, questioningly, before he interrupted.

"Come on then, man. Open it up."

Again, I did as I was told, passing it over to him.

He took a swift swig, before screwing his face up as if he'd been shot in the stomach, his face a picture of agony and bewilderment. I did the same as he passed it back to me, but with less of a face to go with it.

I knew that it was wrong, it began to soothe me as it burned away at my insides. It was as if it were some sort of concoction that held magical qualities for me, that helped to steady my mind as much as it helped steady my hand. It also had the added side effect of beginning to eat away at the pounding headache that had been plaguing me for what felt like hours.

As I screwed the lid back on, making sure it was tight and secure, so that I wouldn't lose a single drop of it, the Captain finally pulled himself together again and spoke.

"Pass the message along, Sergeant. Prepare to move."

I passed the message on personally, as if I was acting as the Captain's spokesman for his endeavours. Each man responded in the affirmative with varying degrees of confidence and fear. All of them, except for Bob, who glared at me as if he was still genuinely annoyed with me.

He must have spotted the Captain and I sharing a drink at the front of our column. We were about to go to war; we were about to undertake something that had a less than zero chance of survival. In my mind, he really needed to get his priorities straight.

Now that I had a clear head, I started to reconsider my motivations for why I wanted him out of the team, and realised that maybe it wasn't out of an act of love, and for his own preservation, but so that I could have an easier ride every time I whipped the hip flask out in my moment of need.

As I brushed past Earnshaw, he gripped my arm and muttered something.

"You know, a good sergeant would share that with his men," he had a broad smile sweeping across his face. He needed to lose the smile as soon as possible, the brightness of his perfect white teeth in amidst the darkness was threatening our lives.

"Yeah well, I am not a good sergeant."

I hadn't intended it as a joke, but out of the serious

underlying doubt that I had myself. Nevertheless, Earnshaw and McKay, who had both been within earshot, found the whole thing uproariously funny and continued to suppress snorts and chuckles as they removed the safety catches on their rifles.

It felt good to have a rifle back in my hands and know that its efficiency and stopping power would be put to good use in a few minutes' time. It was like not seeing a trusted friend or relative for many months, but then reacquainting yourself with them, as if it hadn't been that long ago since you had last seen them.

I suddenly had the thought that, apart from my hip flask, my rifle was the only real friend I could depend on in this war. It was the only one that I could trust my life with.

We moved away from the smoking cigarettes by the artillery pieces, and began to move further west, so that we could intersect the light railway line further up the track. We scampered around cautiously, stopping every few hundred yards or so to doublecheck that the men at the artillery battery hadn't put out some kind of alert that they had seen us.

But that was one advantage of being the very first men to go this far into enemy lines; the Germans weren't expecting our presence at all.

The railway track itself afforded us a surface that was far firmer than the rickety old duckboard pathways that we had got used to over the last few miles. It allowed for us to move far quicker than before, and with a greater assurance that we were heading in the right direction, something which had played on my mind ever since the plan was initially put to us.

The track was certainly able to provide a much more stable platform for us to run on, and one that meant that we didn't have to worry about the boggy fields that surrounded the entire place which, despite the dry weather that we had enjoyed recently, still had enough water on the surface to quench the thirst of an entire village.

I recalled a small nugget of information that I had gleaned from the ever-knowledgeable Sergeant Hughes, about how this whole area was built on clay, which made water incredibly difficult to seep through the surface of the earth. It turned out that I had listened to him far more often than I had ever imagined.

We journeyed on uneventfully, for what felt like tens of miles; my unprepared body creaking and cracking in refusal to go on much further. But I simply had to, I had to think of what it might mean to those men if we were to silence the guns even for a day.

The area around us suddenly became even more populated than before, and even the odd tree untouched by war defiantly stood out of the landscape.

That meant that we were out of range of British artillery, which meant we couldn't be too far away from our intended target.

I became like an impatient child, who wanted everything and couldn't understand why they had to wait for it. I began to dream of what the supply dump looked like, and even began to see it through the wall of darkness that we continued to charge through.

Then, quite suddenly, my apparitions became a reality and I had to rub my eyes to check that I was seeing what it was I thought I saw.

But it was, it definitely was. It was the supply dump, our intended target.

I began to experience the feelings of jubilation and satisfaction that I had warned myself against so many other times before, my visions turned from what the supply dump might look like once we had finished with it.

Don't get ahead of yourself. This is far from over.

We all stopped about four hundred yards from where the railway track ended, and the supply dump began. Clutching our rifles to our chests, as if they were innocent children, we crouched behind an abandoned truck, that had clearly become bogged down by all the water. It was still in a relatively good condition, but the underside had started to rust ever so slightly, on account of the fact that it had been perched there, forgotten, for an indeterminable amount of time.

"Well, here we are boys. This is the target. You remember your briefing, don't do anything stupid, just stick to what you know. We regroup here immediately after we have left, alright? Stay safe."

The Captain bowed his head after his little speech, either in a moment of contemplation or prayer. I couldn't discern which.

"We've made it this far, lads. Don't let it slip, we do what we came here to do and nothing else. Even if that means we sacrifice ourselves for the good of the objective. Understood?"

They all began nodding.

We observed the supply dump for a few minutes, taking in what obstacles we might find and men that might put up a fight against us.

It was difficult to make out in the dark, but one soldier made the fatal error of lighting a match and lifting it to his face.

We took that as our signal to move. It was a small window, but it was one that meant we knew where one of our enemies were, and we simply couldn't pass up on such an opportunity.

We advanced slowly as a group, rifles swaying threateningly around our hips to project an image of passivity and friendliness, in case he saw us too soon.

But he didn't. Within seconds, McKay had appeared behind him and by the time we had reached him, Fritz was coolly stubbing out the German's cigarette for him as he lay silently in the dirt.

Almost casually, we walked into the supply dump.

14

We walked into the supply dump as if we owned the place, heads held high, shoulders back and rifles slung over our shoulders. We needed desperately to seem like we belonged, like we knew why we were there.

Having said that, we all kept our revolvers drawn and our other weapons very close by, just in case we were seen for the frauds that we were and had to shoot a way out of the situation.

The supply dump itself was very poorly protected, with only a few sentries wandering aimlessly up and down the large corridors, that were formed by the stacked-up crates and boxes that lined the camp itself. Each one of the sentries that sauntered past us didn't seem like they could care any less for what they were protecting, and that they didn't care who was to wander into the camp.

Which was good news for us, as we wanted all of it, and having some unfocused sentries on duty made our job a lot easier than if they were switched on.

As we staggered deeper and deeper into the supply dump itself, I could make out different boxes of varying shapes and sizes marked with stencilled letters that I couldn't translate. But for the most part, I didn't need to, because there seemed to be absolutely everything that the German army could ever desire here.

There was crate upon crate of machine gun ammunition, hidden under a heavy tarpaulin, with enough rounds to wipe out every soldier in the British Army. Under another tarpaulin, was thousands of rounds of rifle cartridges, each one ready and waiting to be allocated to a German soldier that would eventually be fired towards British men.

There were even one or two boxes of brand-new rifles, a couple of them even equipped with marksman's sights, the likes of which I had never seen before on a British rifle. We ear-marked those crates for demolition, so that we could potentially save even more British lives and chip away at the Germans' morale even further.

There seemed to be everything they could ever wish for in the supply dump, but for a moment we didn't think we would find where our true target was. That was until, however, Hamilton found a large wooden storage facility, designed to keep the artillery shells dry.

We had successfully located our target for the evening.

Once we had found where the main bulk of the artillery shells were, we were completely ecstatic, behaving like schoolchildren who'd found out that school had been closed forever.

"Who would have thought, eh?" whispered McKay, so softly that he wouldn't have even woken a new-born baby.

"Over No Man's Land, into their frontline, through their network and all the way out here. And we're all still alive."

But now was not the time to congratulate ourselves, we needed to remain on task, we needed to remain focused.

"Stop. Check yourselves, this is where men die. I want to get as many of you back to our frontlines as possible tonight."

I had never liked the hard-nosed NCO role that so often accompanied three stripes on a man's arm, and it was something that I had actively avoided since I had been promoted from a private. I had taken up the laissez-faire attitude of letting the team get on with whatever they wanted to do and with minimal interference from above. But tonight, something changed within me, I no longer felt like the NCO who didn't care about his men and only about himself, but I felt like a father to these boys, like they were an integral part of my family and wanted them around for as long as was humanly possible.

"Yes. I agree with the Sergeant. Don't get ahead of yourselves. We still have a long way to go."

The Captain spoke quietly, but firmly, with the kind of tone that everyone knew not to argue with. He looked to me to issue the rest of the instructions.

"Right, you all have your allocated sectors. Make sure you wait for the prearranged signal, a lot hinges on that. Stay low, stay quiet, and make sure you stay in the shadows. They could get you killed, but they can also help you live.

"Has anyone got any questions? Has anyone lost their explosives?"

Everyone began checking their satchels hastily, and in turn returned reports to me by a quick shake of the head. They were ready. I was ready. We could get this job done.

"Right then," grumbled the Captain, "to your duties. Good luck gents."

He looked at each member of his team in turn, staring at us, before nodding his head gently, which unnerved me a little bit. He had never done anything like that before, it had always been a simple issuing of orders before getting on with them. But, this time, forebodingly, he was saying goodbye.

We slowly dissipated into the night, clutching to the shadows that were produced by the towering wooden crates that had been stacked as high as the Germans dared. We each made our way to our designated sector, a long line of supplies each that we would be responsible for getting rid of.

The Captain and I had the most important task, the one which we had set out to achieve; the artillery shells. Outside the wooden shelter the others were all dancing around in the darkness, placing their ammonal-packed tins to anything that would go bang.

Based on the sheer amount of ordnance that was there, and all the other things that were vaguely flammable, there was a very good chance that this whole place was going to be ablaze in a matter of moments.

The explosive-packed tins had been modified especially for us, with a new fuse that would allow us a little bit more time to get away than usual. Even so, I had reservations about how helpful a ten-minute time delay would actually be in this situation.

But, as I made my way around the room, placing the tins in easily accessible positions, I realised that I was getting ahead of myself once again. There was no guarantee that I was going to make it back at all tonight, and even toyed with the idea that going out in an almighty explosion might be the best way for me to go.

At least that way I wouldn't know so much of the pain of a bullet wound or a bayonet thrust.

As I placed the last of my explosives underneath the tarpaulin of another crate of shells, I chanced a quick look at my wristwatch. It was one thirty-three in the morning, and I was beginning to get another headache.

I couldn't quite work out whether it was the intense tiredness that was exhausting my ability to stay pain-free, or if it was the fact that I was desperate for another quick swig from the hip flask.

So, I put my theory to the test and pulled the flask from my top pocket. It was only as I took a swig, that I realised how cold my skin was and how much pain the icy night was causing me. Being aware of the serious need to stay warm I pushed the hip flask back into my pocket and withdrew my packet of Navy Cut cigarettes.

I put one in my mouth and let it dangle there for a moment, while I made my way to the entrance of the temporary warehouse that I was in. Even I wasn't stupid enough to light a cigarette that close to what must have been a month's supply of high explosive artillery shells.

It appeared that neither was Captain Arnold, because as soon as I rounded the corner to get to the door, his tall, imposing figure was already standing there, a small glowing stick hanging from his mouth.

"Keeping watch. Thought it might make me look more German."

"It's not really working, if I may say so, Sir."

He looked at me with a smirk, "Okay then, it's just so terribly cold tonight."

"You're not wrong, Sir."

He lit my cigarette for me, and we spent the next few minutes staring out of the big barn door, gazing at everything that was around us. I couldn't quite believe that we had made it this far. We were now standing, quite nonchalantly, five miles behind the German frontline, in one of their supply dumps.

It was almost impossible to believe. But here we were.

"You know, I always fancied myself to become a locomotive driver one day," I rasped in between drags on my cigarette. The Captain gave me a quizzical look, "the light railway… You reckon the Germans would mind if I took it for a ride?"

The Captain chuckled for a moment, ignoring my question. He didn't think I was serious.

"It is not all that it is cracked up to be, Ellis. My father invested heavily in the development of British locomotives. It is hard work to drive one. It is not a glamorous life."

"Your father, the Earl of Somewhere?"

It had been a burning question ever since it had been mentioned when I first arrived in the team. A leading member of the British aristocracy, now in charge of a humble trench raiding team. It had been up there with the other myths of the section, like why Sergeant Hughes had been kicked out of the clergy.

I had missed my chance to find out about that one, so I was determined to make sure I closed this one down before the Captain was killed.

"He's not quite an Earl exactly."

"Then, what is he?"

"My father is only a Baron. But we are closely related to an Earl. Earl Grey."

"Like the tea?"

"Yes, exactly like the tea. Named after one of my uncles, I believe."

Simultaneously, we stubbed our cigarettes out on the floor, tucking them under a stack of crates nearby, just to try and hide our presence from the eagle-eyed German who might suddenly come snooping.

This was a curious war, one that had killed men but made others, and led to a young man, who was to be trained as a baker, sharing a cigarette with a man who would almost certainly be on first name terms with the Prime Minister's Cabinet. I couldn't help but smirk to myself, as the choking fumes of our cigarettes slowly surrendered to the crispness of the midnight air.

"Do you miss it, Sir?"

"My name is Terence, Andrew. Terry when the others are not around. Try and get used to that, would you? Hughes was good at remembering that. It makes me feel a little bit more human. A little less invincible. You know how it is."

"Yes, Sir...Terry. Of course."

It felt strange to me, to now have a friend of such a

high standing, who I was able to share a cigarette with and have a normal conversation. The premise of having a normal friend had gone out of the window the minute that I had first gone over the top, and I had a strange, warm feeling in the pit of my stomach.

The fact that the Captain wanted to humble himself to my social standing and to make himself feel less invincible, gave me great courage to know that I was fighting with this man. He knew that the Germans cared not for his titles or father's peerage, and that from the sights of a rifle, one man looked exactly the same as the other. He was at just as much of a risk as we were.

"Yes, I do."

"Pardon?"

"Miss my life. From before. It was a good life. Probably not one that you would have experienced, but nevertheless, it was a good life. I can barely remember what it was like now. It feels so long ago, when in actual fact, I only joined the army two years ago now."

I began to think of my own home and how my life would have compared to his. It was difficult to recall what I had done growing up, the faces of my friends now nothing more than a faded silhouette in the darkest corners of my own memory.

I did miss it, but I had no direct reasons why, I struggled to pinpoint an exact reason why I wanted to go home. I was in danger out here, but I had finally found something that I enjoyed and for the first time in my life, I had found something that I was actually quite good at.

In a way, I didn't want to make it home.

I had made some incredible friends in the short war that I had experienced, one of them being Bob Sargent, who had become more of an enemy in recent weeks. But I still cared for him, I still wanted him by my side deep down.

The only real reason why we had erupted into ferocious arguments was because I knew that he was right. I had shot him as a result of my own dependence on the paraffin. I had known it for a while now, it had become the one thing that I was craving every minute of every day. It was probably why I had a stinking headache as I was stood talking to the Captain.

I resolved there and then to apologise to him, the minute that this was all over, and ask for his forgiveness for everything that I had said and done. The scar that was now permanently on his skin, would have to act as a constant reminder as to why I was trying to cleanse myself of all the foibles that I had picked up along the way.

I noticed however, that I refrained from pouring the contents of the hip flask out on the ground right there and then. I might still need it tonight at least.

"Do you have anything left in that hip flask, Sergeant?"

It was as if Captain Arnold had been reading my mind. I smiled at him weakly, vaguely reaching in the direction of my pocket, preparing to unbutton it, whilst still keeping my gaze outwards, around the supply dump for any movement that should not have been there.

Before I could reply, and before I could free the hip flask from my pocket, there was an almighty boom in the distance. I felt it ripple under my feet for just a moment, but it didn't really grab my full attention. I was still ever so slightly worried that I might have spilled some of my paraffin.

We both looked at each other, that was our signal. We wouldn't be sharing another sip from the hip flask for the time being.

15

I gazed at the Captain for a fraction of a second too long, before turning my head towards the noise to avoid the ongoing staring contest that we had locked ourselves into. I had nothing in particular to look at, apart from the mountains of darkened silhouettes as the crates seemed to climb to the sky in every direction.

I could feel Captain Arnold's eyes burning into the side of my face as we both continually asked ourselves the same question, over and over.

Was that it? Was that our signal?

"Do you think that was it?" Captain Arnold managed to grumble in the intervening second immediately after the faint rumbling noise.

It had emerged like a roll of thunder, not the immediate and explosive eruption that I had expected, but a low rumble, followed by a more aggressive and meaningful bellow. It had come from the west of our position, or the easier reference point for us all to make, from the direction of the frontline.

It must have been what we had been waiting for, it simply had to be. Or had I misheard it? Maybe it had just been an artillery salvo landing in the distance, and both the Captain and I had been so preoccupied with talking to each other that we hadn't heard it correctly.

But then, just as I was rebuking myself for being so inattentive, the ground at my feet began to shake. It was more of a quiver and, for a moment, I reached for my hip flask to try and calm myself down, as it felt like I had entered some sort of full body trance at the lack of alcohol that was in my system.

Just as I moved my hand up to reach it, I realised that Captain Arnold had felt it too.

"That was it," he declared, a menacing grin etching itself across his face. I returned it, thankfully lowering my hand as it meant that I wasn't quite as ill as I thought I was.

I'll get rid of it, all of it. As soon as I'm back. If I make it back.

We nodded to one another, as we both put a cigarette to our lips and lit them simultaneously, as if we were both looking into a mirror.

I hope everyone else was as unsure as we were.

If we had been the last ones to realise that the rumble was in fact our signal to move, then there was a possibility that explosions would begin erupting all around us, before we even had the chance to light our fuses.

Ciggies now glowing ominously in the dark, we both pulled ourselves back into action.

"Good luck, Ellis."

"You too, Sir. Sorry, Terry."

He smirked at me once more, before darting away to

where he had placed his explosives. Without wasting another half a second, I did exactly the same.

The tins began to hiss away violently, far louder than I had ever heard them before, as I convinced myself that within seconds an entire German garrison would be hot on our heels to go and put them out.

My body groaned as I pushed myself to run faster and harder than I ever had done previously. We really didn't have all that long to light the explosives, get out of the barn and the supply dump before the world around us exploded into a fireball.

It really was going to be close.

I skidded round the last corner of wooden boxes as I hared towards the entrance to the barn. Launching my cigarette into the nearest stash of anything I could see, I spun my rifle off my back, to prevent it from clobbering me around the back of my skull and knocking me out.

It also meant that I would be able to run faster, which would a bonus right now.

I began to stretch my legs as far as they would possibly go, feeling so fast that I began to think I could overtake myself and that within a flash, I would be head over heels and lying face down in the dirt, but it never happened.

"Andrew!" screamed a voice, as a figure stumbled out of the shadows. "Andrew! Over here!"

By the time my brain had processed the voice, I was within spitting distance of the supply dump boundary and I could even see the body of the dead German sentry as he continued to stand guard at his posting.

Bob was further back from me and the thought crossed my mind that I should leave him, it was every man for himself now, the Captain had said as much. But there was something in his voice, something that I had never detected until that point.

He had a gravelly grain to his speech, like he was always trying to cough up a ball of phlegm, but as he continued to call out my name, there was a desperation to it, a timidity hidden amongst it. He was scared, fearful.

You have to go back for him. He's your friend.

I turned, almost half-heartedly, as I observed the silhouette that came staggering towards me. He was perhaps one hundred yards from where I was, a deviation of a precious few seconds that I simply did not have.

I had less than thirty yards to go until I made it to the rusting wagon that we had passed on our way in, its promise of some sort of cover and safety luring me away from my longest-serving comrade.

I stumbled for a moment or two, deciding which way to turn, every second I wasted doing nothing to help me get back alive.

"Andrew! It's my stitches," he screamed at me, caring not an inch about who might hear us. It was too late for that anyway. "They've come undone!"

It was then that I realised that he was dabbing away as best he could at his side, the hole that had been opened up by one of my own rounds re-emerging between his bloodied hands. The pangs of guilt began to wash over me again.

As I went to catch the stumbling figure, blood gushing from his side, flecks of dirt began to dance around my feet.

It did not take me long to recognise the accompanying pops of a rifle to tell me that we had been found out. Immediately, I blamed Bob's thoughtless screaming.

The rounds continued to whistle away either side of me, or thwack into the ground, which meant that I was either up against some very blind Germans, or they were still on the move. Maybe both.

"Move!" screamed another voice, so loud that it sounded as if the screaming was inside my very own head. "I've got him! Go! Go!"

Earnshaw's silhouette, his fair-haired and slimline frame bent over, his head spurring him on, suddenly appeared from behind Bob. He was in safe hands. Now all I had to do was give them a meagre chance at surviving the next twenty seconds.

I turned and ran towards the blinking lights of rifle fire.

16

I thundered to the vehicle, that seemed so out of place in the middle of this war, that I thought it would disappear at any moment. Thankfully, it didn't, and I managed to slam myself into its steely exterior, shortly before the Germans made it to the other side.

They had advanced slowly, taking their time over the shots but still moving too fast to group them properly. I, on the other hand, dipped my head as if in some sort of mocking bow, and threw one limb in front of the other, barely breathing until I made it to the safety of the truck.

I had no time to catch my breath or indeed begin to take any in at all, as I was already setting myself up to knock back the three enemy soldiers that had now turned their attention to the limping duo, just fifty yards behind me.

They were moving slowly, methodically, as if they were trying not to spill too much on the German's ground out of courtesy. But they also moved with an urgency, one that meant Bob continued to lose blood the more he stumbled around.

There were three flashes from what I could see, each of them erupting in what appeared to be synchronised volleys as they advanced.

Flash. Flash. Flash. Pause. Flash. Flash. Flash.

I barely hesitated in aiming half an inch above where the central flash had come from, quickly firing off a couple of rounds either side, to scare the others into thinking that I was coming for them next.

It worked. The other two flashes began to erupt far less frequently, from somewhere much lower to the ground than where they had been before.

They had no cover anywhere near them, their best option of defence would be to turn and run the other way. But they were brave men.

I wondered who they thought we were and what we were doing. Maybe they knew straight away that we were British soldiers, or maybe the possibility was going through their minds that we were deserters, trying to shorten the war by sabotaging our own supplies.

Either way, it didn't really matter too much. The fact was that they were firing at me and all I needed to focus on was responding back in kind.

It took another five rounds to make sure that the flashes stopped, although I had no way of confirming whether I had actually hit the men, or if they had simply scarpered.

"Go, Ellis! Go! Move on ahead, clear the way!" Earnshaw screamed at me, hoarsely, his strong northern tones just as humorous to my ears as they had been the first time that I had heard them.

He was comforting me in a way, it felt good to know that there was someone quite literally behind me, urging me forward. But, at the same time, I knew that if I was to turn against his advice, he would be the first to put a bullet in me.

I had no idea where the Captain, McKay and Hamilton were, no knowledge even if they were still alive or not. It was possible that I had become the point man for which half the German army would be wanting to exact their revenge upon.

I thundered over the duckboards, making far more noise than an express train ever could, and I thought about how vastly different our withdrawal had been compared to our infiltration. Just over an hour ago, I had been lying face down in the mud on either side of the duckboards, silently hoping that the Germans would not discover my presence.

Now, I was making as much noise as possible, firing the odd round from my rifle at my hip, in the hope that the few soldiers that were around thought there might be many more of us than the six that were now scattered behind the lines.

It felt like hours before I began to recognise certain aspects of the countryside as being close to the German lines. Progressively, the lay of the land seemed to get flatter and flatter, until the point where it seemed like I was the only living thing above the ground.

Every now and then, I half turned, making sure that both Earnshaw and Bob were behind me. Either Bob had been faking it, or he was digging deep, as they were both keeping up with me tremendously well.

Suddenly, the cracks of rifles sparking up somewhere

behind me began to sound, as the whistling of close rounds began to whisper either side of my head. Instinctively, I charged on further, with no feelings of guilt or duty to turn and help Bob and Earnshaw.

I skidded to a halt when I saw the flickers of light sparkle directly ahead of me, as a group of even more rifles began to bark away at the figures charging towards them.

The bangs and hisses grew to an almost unbearable level, as the walls began to close in on either side of me.

I was trapped. The only way I could go would be left or right, and I would be no closer to home either way.

I resigned myself to defeat. I should have expected it after all. The plan had been an audacious one, to say the least, but I felt hard done by, nonetheless. For some reason, I truly believed that I deserved to make it through the war, or through the night at the very least.

I stood perplexed, just waiting for the fateful round to catch me and penetrate one of my vital organs. It wasn't a question of if it might happen, but when. The only question that seemed to linger over me unanswered was from which side the round would come from.

What would you prefer? In your front? Or your back?

"Ellis!" a voice suddenly bawled straight ahead of me, "Move! What are you doing, man?!"

It was the Captain. I would have recognised his voice from a thousand yards away. The blinking flashes of rifles that I had seen at my twelve o'clock had been my friends. Captain Arnold, McKay and Hamilton had somehow got ahead of us.

Maybe I will get back.

"Get over here, Andrew! Now!" McKay was definitely there.

As their voices assaulted my ears the bullets from behind seemed to intensify, as if they were trying to keep up with the cacophony of noise that lay ahead.

I didn't feel quite so trapped anymore.

Help Bob, then. Help Earnshaw. Come on.

I spun round, my right knee smacking into the duckboards so hard that I felt the wood begin to splinter under my weight. I had men behind me to cover my back, I was more helpful to Bob and Earnshaw if I was firing.

As their heads bobbed up and down, their limbs doing much the same, I caught the unmistakable muzzle flashes of rifles from a hundred yards behind them, but they were closing in fast.

I could not tell how many of them there were, but if they kept it up, it didn't matter. Eventually, they would be firing point blank.

"Ellis! What are you doing? Over here!"

"Andrew, move! Don't be so stupid!"

I didn't know what had come over me. I suddenly recalled all of my selfish moments, every single one, not just since I had arrived in France.

It was the first time that I had given any real consideration to my family, as I silently thanked my parents for everything that they had done for me. I began to mutter a thanks to Bob too, who had backed me up to everyone that he had ever met. It had only been a slight hiccup that had made us fall out and I felt awful for it.

I thought about Sergeant Needs and how he had selflessly given himself up, how everyone in that section had, all for me. It was about time that I began to pay them back and it seemed only right that I should start with Bob.

My rifle felt heavy and awkward in my grip, as if it had taken on a new meaning for me. I wasn't killing for my own self preservation now, I was doing it for someone else.

I heaved it up, as if it was the only thing that could redeem me now as I peered down the sights.

I could make out the lumbering figures of Bob and Earnshaw, but also the fainter shadows of the men that were giving chase.

One or two of them had dropped to a knee to fire off some well-aimed shots, but quickly gave up as their targets moved with an extraordinary speed.

As if my attention continued to gravitate back towards Bob, my sights found their way onto his chest more than once.

Blood was now pouring from his side, but he appeared as though he was beyond the point of caring. He just wanted to get back alive. Or maybe it was Earnshaw's refusal to let go of him.

I applied a miniscule amount of pressure to the trigger, as another German crouched to one knee to have another pop. But a flash of red caught my eye, making me relinquish my grip around the curved steel.

It was blood. Bob's blood.

The night where I had hit him replayed itself in my mind and I was forced to watch him cartwheel down to the ground, like a sycamore seed as it pirouetted to the earth.

I had hit him once before. And now it was that very

same wound that was slowing him down. I couldn't pull the trigger. I didn't want to miss again.

Either way, it would be me who was the one who had got Bob Sargent killed.

My hands moved far too slowly as I bit down hard on my back teeth, letting out a low growl as I watched the Germans edge ever closer to them.

I squeezed and squeezed, the echoing of the round ejecting completely eclipsed by my bellow that roared from the depths of my lungs.

Bang.

I opened my eyes.

I hadn't hit Bob, but I hadn't hit the Germans either.

They had all dropped to one knee however, as if the first sign of resistance had been all that was needed to get them off Bob's back.

"Fire!" roared the Captain from behind me, as the other rifles began to spark up some sort of meagre reply to the pursuing Germans.

I fired my rifle again. And again.

Soon, it was time to reload. But it was too late. The Germans were getting far too close. If I wanted to have any hopes of surviving the night, I would need to move, and sharpish.

Bob and Earnshaw were now less than thirty yards from me, but the Germans were probably only the same distance from them.

What are you going to do, Andrew? Decide. Now.

As I fumbled around, blindly reloading the rifle that I had learnt how to operate blindfolded, Bob suddenly looked up from his stooped posture and locked eyes with me.

It was the worst thing that he could have done.

The quiver in my hand took hold with a renewed vigour and purpose, to prevent me from making my rifle operational again.

Tears began forming up in my eyes as I stared at him solemnly, silently communicating to one another.

In subsequent dreams his words had ranged from, "It's okay Andrew, go," to "Why did you leave?" My response always remained the same, "I'm sorry, Bob. I'm sorry."

I hoped, as he continued to glare at me, that he knew how truly sorry I was. Not just for the wound that was now holding him back, but for everything. For putting him in the position where he felt like I was threatening his own safety as well as my own. For making him bear the burden of extra responsibility as the only NCO who was sober, the only one who was approachable to everyone else.

It was all down to one thing.

GRHMN.

Just as soon as we get back, I will get rid of it.

"Go, Ellis! Get out of here, get to cover!"

I had almost forgotten that Earnshaw was in amongst us.

The Germans behind had dropped to one knee again, all of them this time, as I watched the whites of their eyes narrow as they lined up their shots.

It was time for me to go. There was still a chance that I could make it to the sandbags, where the Captain was, and be of more use to them there. There was a slight possibility that in thirty seconds, they might still be alive.

The flickering glares returned, this time with a more

aggressive fervour, as bits of wooden duckboard threatened to embed themselves into my eyeballs. Instinctively, I turned my head away from them, as more began to flick up and bury themselves in the side of my neck.

"Go, Andrew! Go!"

The lethal splinters that began to spin wildly around me was the only incentive that I needed to break my gaze away from Bob and, once I had done that, I became more like myself again.

As I felt the hot dribbles of blood begin to trickle down my neck and onto my collar, I spun around and ran for the sandbags that began to flash more than a candle in a breeze.

17

I felt like bursting into tears even before I made it to the comfort of the sandbag wall. The wall itself was about three-foot-high and housed behind it three concerned, timid looking faces.

"Weapon up, Ellis. Come on. We need you now."

Hamilton turned away from me, his rifle facing in the opposite direction to the Captain's and McKay's. He was covering our backs, in case any fleeing Germans suddenly popped up out of the ground.

My rifle felt heavier than ever before, as if it had become a burden to me rather than a blessing. Nevertheless, it was up and in my shoulder moments after Captain Arnold had ordered it into action.

"The explosives...They should have gone by now, right?"

"Should have done," I croaked weakly, the thirst tripping every word that came tumbling from my mouth.

"Then what's happened?" screamed McKay, in a

panic, his usual calm and reassuring demeanour thrown away to the side.

"Calm down, McKay," uttered Captain Arnold, in his soothing but firm voice, "It'll come. Just keep laying down some fire."

The rifles either side of me began to crack, firing shots off in pairs and managing to expertly guide the bullets around the two-headed figure, that still defiantly stumbled towards us. I fumbled around with the bolt on my own weapon, but I couldn't get it to slide back forwards. It was jammed.

My hands were shaking violently as I tried my hardest to unblock the jammed round that was refusing to work its way into the breech. I slapped the bolt three or four times, trying to dislodge the round, which did nothing for me.

I slid down behind the wall, pushing my back up against it, hard, as I felt the first few rounds from the Germans begin to bury themselves on the other side. We didn't have much longer left. Bob and Earnshaw had even less time.

I had to overcome my quaking hands, as I pushed my thumb into the breech and pushed down as hard as I could on the neck of the brass bullet, that was causing me all kinds of grief. Releasing it, I felt it move higher up than it had done before, and the bolt was able to slide home.

Finally, I was ready.

I resurfaced atop the sandbags and pulled my rifle into the aim. I could just about make out the vague features of a man as he ran ever closer to his victims.

My sights lined up perfectly with his face and I took up the first hint of pressure on the trigger and began to squeeze, gently. The more pressure that I applied to the curved steel, the lower my aim got, until the sights fell squarely on the man's chest.

Bang.

He dropped to the floor.

At the same instant that I had pulled the trigger, a huge fireball had erupted some way behind the German's head, as if all the explosives had been patiently waiting for me to pull myself together.

The first fireball seemed to trigger the next and the next, until there was one continuous ball of blazing flames rolling around on the horizon. I couldn't tell if it was the excitement that was coursing through my veins, or if it was the heat of the explosion that began to burn away at my face.

Either way, I couldn't look at it for long, as the intense light that boiled brilliantly scorched my eyeballs. None of us could look at it.

The Germans, however, could do nothing but stare, gifting Bob and Earnshaw a well-needed and deserved additional few seconds to make it back to us.

How we were going to proceed once they had made it to us, I had no idea, but I began muttering under my breath for them to make it.

Come on. Come on. You can do this.

"Keep firing, boys! While they have their backs to us, come on!"

I did as I was told and managed to drop two soldiers before they realised that we were their main concern. By the time that happened, there was only three of the pursuers left standing.

"What are you doing, Ellis! Get back down here!" Arnold bellowed as I pulled myself back over the top of the sandbags, leaving my rifle with him. Feeling naked without a weapon, I found my revolver swinging around at my hip and began loosing off rounds in every direction that I possibly could.

I was close to Bob now. I could tell that he was pleased to see me.

His neck was the only bit of skin that I could see, the rest covered in dirt and charred cork. It was pastel white, like all the colour in his body had been completely pumped from him. The pink pigment of his skin was trailing behind him, the scarlet liquid still defiantly seeping from his side.

He was in a bad way.

"Bob! Look up! Look at me!"

As he did so, he spat a mouthful of saliva at me, bloodied saliva. I looked up into his face and I noticed that his eyes were already rolling around into the back of his head, before he had even fallen to the ground.

The muzzle flashes that had been erupting behind him, had finally caught up with him. By the time he finally slumped into the ground, a geyser of mud splashing upwards as he did so, Bob Sargent was already dead.

As if the whole world had been notified of this terrible news, a low, urgent rumble began to shake the foundations upon which I stood. That must have been the secondary blast from the tunnellers. It had to be.

We were running out of time, we had to leave Bob behind.

"He's gone!" I screamed at Earnshaw, who began to stumble around having been dragged to the ground by Bob's corpse.

"Let's move then!"

Two explosions, one behind and one in front of them, had thrown the Germans so much that they stopped firing for a moment. It was as if they thought it signified the end of the war altogether. But all it did was allow Earnshaw and me to get back behind the safety of the sandbag wall, and for the Captain and McKay to pick off the final few hunters.

"Is everyone okay?"

It was a stupid question to ask, but one that had to be voiced now, in case anyone else was likely to slow us down in the same way that Bob had.

The Captain looked around at each of us in turn, met with steely-eyed glares that told him we no longer felt like men, we simply felt like machines. Emotionless machines.

"Back into the front line then?" I suggested, while we reloaded our various weapons, and withdrew some of the more barbaric ones. In all honesty, I felt more at home with a truncheon in my hand, than a rifle. At least I knew if the truncheon failed to work, it was my own fault.

"Through their frontline, into No Man's Land, back into our frontline. All quite simple really."

Captain Arnold, unexplainedly, was smirking.

As we began to move, I started to contemplate the loss of the only real friend that I had since I became a soldier. Bob had always been the one who was there for me, fighting alongside me, keeping an eye on me. It was only in that moment that I realised that the only reason why I hadn't descended into a pit of alcohol fuelled self-destruction, was because I had always been acutely aware of his presence, and his watchful eye.

Now that he was gone, I had no one regulating me, no one to call me into line if I stepped out. Not even the Captain held that much authority over me.

I was concerned about my own future.

If I hadn't had Bob keeping me in check, who knew how many other of my comrades I would have struck in the line of duty.

It was only then that I realised it had been me who had signed Bob's death warrant. It had been me who had been the one to fire the round striking his side, which had been the wound that had slowed him down so much that he was now no longer with us.

I began to consider myself quite lucky; because of Earnshaw's bravery and stupidity, I quite easily could have had two corpses on my conscience for the rest of my life, so I was fortunate to have just the one.

I had killed Bob, there was no one else to blame. There was no rifle-wielding German who could take more responsibility for the destruction of Bob's life than I could. And it was beginning to weigh heavily on my conscience.

As we weaved in and out of various trenches, not being met with any real resistance other than a few German profanities as we rushed to the front line, I began to feel quite glad of the guilt that I was experiencing. It meant that I was a man again, I was beginning to feel things again, which meant that it was possible that I might just make it through this war after all.

It was that recklessness and carelessness that had sent me towards the hip flask. If I began to fear the death of my teammates, then there was a possibility, admittedly a small one, that I might actually be a better soldier for it.

It felt strange to admit it to myself, but I was glad Bob had been killed.

18

I was convinced that none of us had ever run as fast in our lives, as we sped through the trenches on that night. I knew that it was certainly the case in my life. My legs did not respond to any of the messages from my brain, they just continued to work and pump harder and harder than ever before, as they wanted to make it back to safety, just as much as my own mind did.

As one body, we moved so quickly and efficiently that I became convinced that even if a German soldier did get more than half a second to look at us, by the time that he identified us as enemy soldiers it would be too late. We would be out of sight. It felt as if we were almost haunting the Germans as we wafted our way through their lines, piggybacking off the confusion that the tunnellers had brought upon the Germans.

McKay was up ahead, his small but powerful frame acting as the chisel, blasting through the network of trenches, like he knew it from his childhood. He had a fantastic memory, as I could barely remember the maps that had been laid out on the table in front of us, to help us learn the intricate network of communications trenches and fire bays.

In the event however, it was almost impossible to get lost. Every man and his dog seemed to be charging towards the frontline, where the loud eruption had sounded, and the earth had seemed to lift several hundred feet into the air. No one seem to pay any attention to us; the general assumption must have been that we were on our way to the front line to help dig the poor fellows out who had been trapped in the blast.

That was certainly what we found everyone doing when we arrived at the monumental crater that had been left behind by Collins and the other tunnellers that we had met. I quickly made a mental note to find them on my return, congratulate them and thank them for saving my life.

There seemed to be nothing left of the German trenches to a point, all that filled the void was a huge bowl of disturbed earth, with no signs of human life whatsoever. Apart from the handful of soldiers who had begun to scrabble around in the dirt, searching for their friends, nothing seemed to move in this sector of the frontline.

The dust and the dirt only added to all the confusion, as it lingered in the air like death himself. The cover however, allowed us to masquerade ourselves as saviours, as we began scrabbling down and then up the sides of the bowl as if we were trying to conduct some sort of rescue attempt.

No one gave us a second glance.

The anonymity was the desired effect, the ultimate

goal that would allow us to return home. It was the part of the plan that we had all been the most cynical about, but in the event, it was the part that astounded us the most.

The confusion was utterly complete, no one knew what was going on. I was unsure if anyone really knew what had happened, apart from some sort of asteroid plummeting to the earth in this specific part of the line.

I doubted that the men here even knew that the orange glow on the horizon was in fact their supply dump, and that their artillery would be out of ammunition for quite some time. It was even more unlikely that they had heard about a small band of enemy soldiers behind the lines, and the fact that one of them had now been left behind, drowned in a pool of his own blood.

The chaos, made worse by the occasional shouts of an identified body, allowed us to simply slip back out into No Man's Land, easier than we ever had done before. We were just five men, going over the lip of the hole to see if we could find any survivors there.

Confident that we had not been seen, and that in this sector of the line at least, no one would be keeping watch, we began to spring up, sprinting to the nearest shell hole that we could find, before splashing down into it, to reconvene and get our breath back.

We were all accounted for, each one of the faces that stared back at me displaying varying degrees of exhaustion, anger, relief and bereavement. I took a moment to wonder how my face reflected my own feelings, before putting a stop to it to prevent myself from being distracted too much.

You're not safe yet.

The physical exhaustion that had been etched across Captain Arnold's face of late, was almost completely unrecognisable, an expression of relief and pride now taking its place. I began to take note of how humble a man he was, as he began to wind a dressing around Earnshaw's right arm. It appeared that a glancing wound had opened up the length of his forearm.

Hamilton began to offer around a German water bottle that he had liberated at some point during the night. It felt good to poor the quenching liquid down my throat, but it only left me wanting even more. It felt even more addictive than the paraffin that still resided in my top pocket.

As soon as I am back. I'll get rid of it.

"Are you okay, Sergeant?" He queried as he took the bottle back from my grasp, offering it to McKay. He had a genuine compassion around him, a sincere desire to make sure that everyone was able to perform to the very best of their ability. Maybe he had a degree of selfishness about him, that if one person was not entirely focused on what he was doing, that he himself wouldn't make it back alive. It wasn't the worst motivation to have in a place such as this.

"You had known each other a long time, hadn't you?"

"Yes," I croaked feebly, feeling pathetic at the prospect of being comforted by a rookie soldier. "I was the one that got him killed."

Hamilton began shaking his head, "You mustn't blame yourself, Sergeant. It is war after all, men die."

I began trying to argue with him, before restraining myself. He would never fully understand what had happened, he was just as inexperienced as I was just a couple of months ago.

It felt strange, having been out of breath for so long, that we were now given the opportunity to begin breathing properly again. The smell of smoke and death lingered in the air worse than the smell of a latrine on a hot morning, but the oxygen my body gleaned from within its smoky substance was a blessing.

A sense of security suddenly washed over me, a feeling that I was safe, that I would at least make it through the night. Which was strange, considering I was still out in No Man's Land, but the absence of the constant thumping of artillery, and the rattling of machine guns did wonders to settle my nerves out in the desolate landscape.

At the thought of the lack of exploding ordnance falling around us, I pulled myself to the lip of the hole that we were resting in, just peering inquisitively back towards the German lines, and where Bob would lay for eternity.

The orange hue that had spread over a small part of the horizon, had lost part of its intensity, but even in the gloom I could make out the dark, acrid cloud of smoke that signalled a job well done. The supply dump was burning perfectly and, all things considered, losing Bob was a very small price to pay. Especially when we had become so convinced that we wouldn't even get close to their supplies in the first place.

It *was* a small price to pay, but an expensive one. Bob was a good soldier, but an even better man. Now he was gone, and we would be sent a replacement within the next few days, who would have only a shadow of the experience that Bob had possessed and who would, if he was lucky, take months to get anywhere near Bob's standard of soldiering.

Just as I was beginning to lose my battle with the rising tears in my eyes, I felt a figure sidle up next to me, rubbing shoulders in the process.

"We did well," McKay whispered into my ear, "very well..."

I felt him look across at me, "Bob knew the risks Andrew...We all know the risks. Don't we?"

I looked across at him. I was grateful that I still had him by my side. I knew that he had his troubles in the past, but it felt good to know that there was someone who could see inside my head better than I could myself. He was going to be my ballast, the one that was keeping an eye on me, one that would keep me safe.

I nodded gently.

"Captain says we are moving now. Let's get back to Porky Paul and his awful hospitality, shall we?"

"I want nothing more," I answered, smiling weakly. "Let's go, Fritz."

I reached for the hip flask, once more.

As soon as I get back, it'll be gone.

If I get back.

THE END
Join Andrew Ellis and the other Trench Raiders in 'Take Aim' - Book 4 in the Trench Raiders series. Available on Amazon now!

YOU CAN HELP MAKE A DIFFERENCE

Reviews are one of my most powerful weapons in generating attention for my books.
Unfortunately, I do not have a blockbuster budget when it comes to advertising but
Thanks to you I have something better than that.

Honest reviews of my books helps to grab the attention of other readers so, even if you have one minute, I would be incredibly grateful if you could leave me a review on whichever Amazon store suits you.

Thank you so much.

GET A FREE BOOK TODAY

If you enjoyed this book, why not pick up another one, completely free?

'Enemy Held Territory' follows Special Operations Executive Agent, Maurice Dumont as he inspects the defences at the bridges at Ranville and Benouville. Fast paced and exciting, this Second World War thriller is one you won't want to miss!

Simply go to:

www.ThomasWoodBooks.com/free-book
To sign up!

ABOUT THE AUTHOR

Thomas Wood is the author of the 'Gliders over Normandy' series, The Trench Raiders, as well as the upcoming series surrounding Lieutenant Alfie Lewis, a young Royal Tank Regiment officer in 1940s France.

He posts regular updates on his website
www.ThomasWoodBooks.com

and is also contactable by email at
ThomasWoodBooks@outlook.com

twitter.com/thomaswoodbooks
facebook.com/thomaswoodbooks

Printed in Great Britain
by Amazon